Twitching Heart

Matt Méndez

Berkeley Press
Imprint of
Floricanto Press

Matt Méndez

Berkeley Press is an imprint of Inter American Development, Inc.

Floricanto^M Press

7177 Walnut Canyon Road

Moorpark, California 93021

(415) 552-1879

www. floricantopress. com

ISBN: 978-1480257023

"Por nuestra cultura hablarán nuestros libros. Our books shall speak for our culture. "

Roberto Cabello-Argandoña, Editor

Yasmeen Namazie, Co-editor

Genevieve Miller, Co-editor

Cover art by Mario Robert

Twitching Heart

For Marlo

"In every man there is the possibility of his being—
or, to be more exact, of his becoming once again—
another man."

Octavio Paz, *The Labyrinth of Solitude*

"Y ustedes y yo y todos sabemos que el tiempo
es más pesado que la más pesada carga que puede
soportar el hombre."

Juan Rulfo, *Pedro Páramo, El Llano en Llamas y
Otros Textos*

Contents

Twitching Heart

Chuy didn't believe in miracles. As a boy he prayed Our Fathers and Hail Mary's all the time, even did Novenas in his bedroom, but he never felt what he was supposed to, no fuzzy feelings, no hint that anyone was listening. All he got from praying was sore-as-hell knees.

Teresa called Chuy at work and asked him to stop by the house and watch the boy. Her call was what he'd wanted, a sign she was cooling off, but Chuy couldn't relax as he sat in his old living room and watched TV. He couldn't take the noise as he flipped through the channels; the yelling of judge and preacher shows used to make him laugh, how stupid people could be, but now Chuy felt like the dummy defendant getting abused by the judge. Some embarrassed *pendejo* standing next to a preacher in a slick three-piece suit suddenly in need of saving. Teresa had lost her mind over the affair, taking things too far by tossing him out. She was right to be sangrona, he knew, but Chuy also knew his going had nothing to do with another woman. The trouble was Oscar, their eleven-year-old son.

"Put it on cartoons," Oscar said, sitting in front of the television. He'd been talking about some goofy show, one with wizards and dragons and things that would get the boy labeled a total weirdo. Teresa had dressed him in high-water slacks and a button-up she fastened to the top, his head looking like a light bulb screwed into its socket. His boy should be dressed right, looking sharp in a Dallas Cowboy jersey, maybe some Dodger Blue. As a kid Chuy had imagined himself as the Dodger's closer, cutting fastballs to close out big games, and though he'd only once been to the stadium, the green flat-topped grass and plucking organ music felt like home.

"Does this mean you're coming back, you being here?" Oscar asked, still watching the television. The boy never looked him in the eye, and Chuy didn't know if he was acting afraid or malcriado.

"Soon," he said. "Your má needs some time, so she says, but yeah, I'll be back. You want that, Oscar? Want your *apá* home?"

"Yeah," Oscar said, stealing a glance at Chuy.

Chuy thought Oscar was soft because he carried a layer of fat around his waist and face, because he was a crybaby. Teresa tried to convince him that there was nothing wrong with their son; the extra weight would shed during puberty, and he was sensitive, that's all. She scolded Chuy for forcing Oscar to join Little League even though the boy blew it off, getting stuck in right field and refusing to take his turns at bat, the ball too scary for him. Chuy went to all the games, yelling through the loose chain link fence for Oscar to get in the game and show some heart, but Oscar never did, not like when Chuy pitched the hard and inside stuff to finish off opposing teams in high school. The boy only did what Teresa wanted him to.

"Can you please put it on cartoons?"

Chuy switched the television to the all-cartoon channel. A photograph of Teresa and Oscar eating in the park hung on the wall. They smiled from behind the glass. Plastic roses sprouted from vases on the coffee and mismatched end tables, a puffy slipcover on the sofa. The room looked nice, "girlie," and Chuy had to look hard for signs he'd once lived there. Sloppy patches in the drywall, a cigarette burn on the carpet, the ceramic horses he'd bought Teresa on her thirty-first birthday were the only bits left.

"Má said you were supposed to heat up dinner," Oscar said. "I could do it myself, but she doesn't trust me with the oven."

"Your má don't trust no one," Chuy said, remembering the night she booted him. The lines on her face had creased around her eyes and mouth like cracks on a slab of concrete. She'd been pissed, and he'd felt bad for Teresa, her turning old like that.

"Who don't I trust?"

She came in the living room wearing her shapeless blue dress and pointy low-heeled shoes, her church clothes. Oscar ran to Teresa and wrapped himself around her leg. She eyeballed Chuy. He wore his normal work clothes, a dusty pair of coveralls splattered with paint and plaster, crusted concrete along the bottoms.

"Mamá, I'm hungry," Oscar said. "*Apá* didn't heat the food."

"Chuy, how could you forget dinner?

"N'hombre, I didn't know what time you were

getting back. I'll do it next time."

"Don't be so sure about next time."

"I said I was sorry."

"You're always saying sorry. Just do things right for once."

The conversation would turn bad if Chuy kept at it. Teresa had landed a job answering phones for some doctor, probably thought it was a big deal, but he was glad she'd taken the jale. Teresa needed to see how things went outside the house. The world could wear a man down if he hadn't learned to be tougher than the job he was working, but Chuy also needed to prove he could watch Oscar while Teresa learned this important lesson. Then maybe she would let him raise Oscar like a man.

"If I moved back, I could watch him better. You know, get back in the flow of things."

"I don't want to talk about it."

"I could sleep on the sofa."

"Go and get ready," Teresa said to Oscar, ignoring Chuy. "We'll pick up something after we meet the new neighbors." Oscar sighed and shuffled to his room.

"What new neighbors?" Chuy asked.

"A woman and her daughter down the street."

"No husband, huh?" Chuy wondered if she were making them up.

"Maybe they like it better that way," Teresa said, eyeballing him again.

Chuy wanted to say something but all he did was shrug. He could never talk quick like her, be the first to say something smart. Teresa told him about the new neighbors. They were faith healers from somewhere in California and ended up in El Paso, in Central no less. Moved into the empty Téllez house. The woman's name was María, her daughter, Angélica.

"I could go with you guys, take a look around. Maybe I could help out with some repairs on that old dump, welcome her right." Chuy said, seeing his chance to show Teresa he was trying to be better.

Teresa studied him. Chuy remembered how fine she used to be—her thin nose barely holding her glasses and slightly crooked teeth that flashed when she smiled. She was once all he wanted, and he couldn't believe how messed up everything had become.

"If you want," she finally said.

The old Téllez house wasn't in bad shape, at least not from the outside. Chuy stood on the porch with Teresa and Oscar, the fall evening growing dark from behind clouds. The mellowing heat of the afternoon had slipped away, left the air thin and cold, rainy. Chuy wiped yellow grass and soggy leaves from under his feet. He liked this time of year, things shutting down and taking a break from all the drama.

The house had been abandoned for the past six months, after the Téllez couple died inside—their swamp cooler quit one morning and turned the brick home into an oven, cooked them up. Chuy knew Teresa loved the idea of one day being an old-bird couple like them, but he hated picturing it. On his wedding day, when the priest asked if he would take Teresa for as long as he lived, he imagined Teresa looking like her mother, fat and round like a bucket, walking with a limp. That was the last thing he wanted, but he said yes and knew she would give him the son already poking through her wedding dress.

A woman appeared at the door, a too happy smile on her face. She looked to be in her forties, older than Chuy and Teresa, but dressed younger, sexier with long red fingernails and bottle blond hair flowing toward her low-cut blouse. She invited them in like they were already camaradas.

"¡Hola!" María said. "It is nice to see such a good looking family."

María and Teresa hugged. The living room was cluttered with unpacked boxes and trash bags stuffed with clothes. The walls had a fresh coat of pink paint—a shitty job—and were lined with saints: La Virgen de Guadalupe, San Judas, Martín de Porress, Martín de Caballero, Juan Diego, Santo Niño de Atocha. María walked over to Oscar and squeezed his cheeks, her voice squealing as the boy turned red. She reminded Chuy of a telenovela, good in all the bad ways.

María took Chuy's hand and introduced herself, her fingernails tickling the outside of his palm. Chuy's affair had been with a customer, an old girlfriend who still looked good and promised that he did, too. Chuy shoved his hand in his pocket, not wanting Teresa thinking the wrong thing.

"You do handy work," María said. "I can tell a man by his hands."

"Mostly tile," Chuy said. "When I can find the work."

"¡Ay! I must keep you from my kitchen. The floor is bad, and I'll get embarrassed." María touched his shoulder. Chuy was sure all Teresa had heard was man and hands, his coming turning out to be a stupid idea.

María led them through the living room with its boxes, the dining room with the puke green carpet, her empty bedroom with all the crosses. Chuy kept his distance from María, staying close to Teresa and the boy, listening as they made small talk. He reminded himself of a stray dog. The tour ended in the kitchen and Chuy glanced at the floor. There were gouges in the laminate—some all the way to the slab.

"I thought you had a daughter?" Oscar asked, breaking the silence. "Mamá said she was sick. Did she die?"

"*Cállate*," Chuy said, grabbing Oscar's arm. Teresa sighed, like he was the embarrassing one. Chuy let go. Teresa had never mentioned anything about a sick or dying girl. He wondered what else Teresa had kept from him; what did Oscar know that he didn't? That's the way things always were between them, always trading secrets.

"It's okay," María said, squatting in front of the boy. "Would you like to meet Angélica? I don't let pilgrims see her this late—she needs her rest, but for you, I'll make the exception." She stood. "For all of you."

Chuy didn't believe in miracles. As a boy he prayed Our Fathers and Hail Mary's all the time, even did Novenas in his bedroom, but he never felt what he was supposed to, no fuzzy feelings, no hint that anyone was listening. All he got from praying was sore-as-hell knees.

"Say yes if you want to," Teresa said.

It was dark inside the room, only the moon lighting the figure beneath a window. Angélica was a young girl, her eyes halfway open, stuck someplace between awake and asleep. Angélica's thick black hair spread over her pillow and dropped onto the floor. The room smelled like melted wax, and Chuy felt like he was in church, except he didn't want to leave.

"Is she okay?" Chuy asked, surprised by his own voice.

"The way God wants her to be," María said. "The only way she can do His work."

Oscar had kept quiet after Chuy picked him up, and Chuy decided to give the boy time to get comfortable. It hadn't been easy to get Teresa to go along with bringing the boy—he'd promised to keep close, take breaks and not let Oscar saw anything. Teresa always worried about Oscar getting hurt, spending too much time on things that wouldn't put him in college. That's our job as parents, she'd always tell him, but the boy needed to know that life wasn't in books. Life got made with strong hands, and only a father could teach that.

Driving through his old neighborhood, past Our Lady of Guadalupe and the Hilltop Barbershop where Old Tony still gave haircuts for seven bucks, Chuy realized how much he loved Chuco, especially in the early morning when nobody was around to see the night thin and the sunrise over the mountains. The spiky bushes and cactuses with flowers blooming on them, sucking up the orange light. He felt his heart open while pulling up to María's, looked over at Oscar; he was asleep, eyes pinched shut. It had taken Oscar twenty-two months to learn to walk but only four to say mamá. Teresa had been so proud, telling Chuy how smart the boy was, how gifted. Chuy left Oscar inside the truck, walked to the house and rang the bell.

"I didn't think you'd be here so early," María said, opening the door. "We're not ready." María didn't look glamorous this time, the skin on her face tugging down like wet sheets on a clothesline. He wondered if he'd woken up Angélica, if that were something she could do. He remembered her arms knotted above her chest like mesquite branches, her frozen face. She'd freaked him out, but he wanted to see her again, had daydreamed about cancers being cured, old ladies in wheelchairs standing and walking around, money found buried in backyards.

"I only got one day with my helper," Chuy said, nodding his head at Oscar. "Gotta finish everything today."

"Entonces," María said, opening the door. "It's good to see a boy learning from his father. That is a special thing."

Chuy and Oscar cleared the kitchen and scrubbed the linoleum with soapy water. When the floor dried Chuy handed Oscar the end of a chalk line and stretched it across the length of the room. A plume of blue dust puffed in the air as he snapped it against the laminate. Oscar surprised Chuy by moving when he did, figuring out where he needed to be and looking for what to do next. "Now the real work starts," Chuy said, cutting open a box of tiles leftover from a job he'd done on the Westside, some *Gringo*'s rec-room that had pictures of his sons hanging on the walls. They smiled in their Coronado T-Bird uniforms and held trophies with little brass baseball dudes on them—trophies lined the wall, too. Chuy remembered thinking how that *Gringo* had it all: money, a good house, a pair of sons who would do him right.

Chuy handed Oscar a tile. "First, you have to check each one for cracks before you set it. Even a small one will bust it apart when the thinset dries." Oscar nodded, and Chuy wondered if he should explain what thinset did, how it hardened and turned little cracks into big ones, but Oscar seemed to understand as much as he needed to.

The sun came up and Chuy stopped to watch the orange light cut through the window. Moved his arm into the rays, wanting to feel warm, but he couldn't regain the hopeful feeling he'd had earlier. This felt like just another job, and he wondered what the hell he'd been thinking. Miracles. How stupid could he be? Oscar sat and checked the tiles for cracks, a pile of empty boxes behind him and a stack of good tiles in front. Chuy never actually checked them. He liked to work fast and most of the time spotted a bad one before setting it—though he sometimes missed and had to fix the mess afterward, but Oscar seemed happy, like he was playing one of his weird games, so Chuy left him to it.

Chuy went to the porch and poured the thinset into a bucket. His knees and back hurt like always, and Chuy felt glad that Oscar was smart and would never have to work like this. But it was the kind of glad that turned rotten by thinking about it; part of him wanted Oscar to end up at a job like his, to show Teresa that nobody's dreams are better because nobody's come true. Chuy added water from the hose and mixed everything until it was thick like peanut butter, lugged it back to the kitchen where he found Oscar standing over the sink.

"It was an accident," Oscar said, pouring water on his hand. "One of the tiles was broken."

"I told you to be careful," Chuy said. Chuy dropped the bucket and grabbed Oscar's hand. A busted tile had gashed him across the palm, and Chuy pressed hard and waited to see if the blood thinned. He heard Teresa's voice in his head: I can't trust you por nada. One day and you cut his hand off.

Oscar stared at his hand and whimpered.

"Don't cry," Chuy said while squeezing, the thin bones of Oscar's hands poking against his fingers. "Don't make it worse."

"I'm not."

Chuy opened Oscar's hand to see how deep the cut

went, and Oscar cried. Chuy thought of hugging the boy the way Teresa did when he was hurt, but he kept squeezing, knowing it wouldn't do any good.

"What's wrong, Oscarcito?" María asked, rushing into the room. She wrapped her arms around the boy.

"I wasn't messing around. I promise," Oscar said between chokes of air.

"Of course you weren't," María said. She calmed Oscar, and Chuy was both jealous and relieved. He'd wanted to tell Oscar that everyone got hurt on the job; his hand would scar, it something he could look back on and remember, better than a picture, because mistakes were real. María went to the cupboard and grabbed a bag of flour, dropped a lump in Oscar's palm and watched as it globed into a reddish ball.

"Make a fist and hold it tight," she said and wrapped his hand in a kitchen towel. "Let me get some orange peels for you to chew on, to stop the bleeding." María disappeared into the dining room.

"Here," Chuy said wrapping the towel tighter around Oscar's fist. "Do you want to call má? I won't get mad."

"No," he said, turning away. "I want to stay with you and finish the job. I don't want you to go again." Teresa would blame Chuy for the hand, say he never looked out for their son. She always told Chuy how Oscar deserved the chance for a better life—the chance they never got, but Chuy knew what Teresa really meant: He deserves better than you.

Chuy wrapped Oscar's hand with a roll of electrical

tape he found at the bottom of his tool bag, going over the kitchen towel until Oscar's hand resembled a black flipper. Teresa would eventually stop by to check on Chuy, overreact and take Oscar away when she saw the hand—probably for good this time. Chuy had flunked her little test and felt bad for thinking about it that way—him losing, them winning, everything fading like old paint.

Getting back to work, Chuy crouched on the floor and spread a glob of thinset with the notched end of his trowel, making even rows across the linoleum. He set the first tile and pressed down, collapsing pockets of air in the thick adhesive. Oscar sat beside him, passing tiles with his good hand and chewing orange peels. María had gone, saying she needed to get Angélica ready for visitors. The house was quiet, and Chuy wondered how Angélica got ready or helped pilgrims.

Oscar passed another tile without saying a word. The boy was still, and for the first time Chuy recognized himself in his son. He had the same slightly open mouth and hard eyes he recognized from the mirror. When Oscar was a baby he'd cried all the time—his lungs like balloons filled with air and then deflating in long shrieks, but that noise had given Chuy hope for the future. Maybe the boy would be one of those marathon runners, gliding across giant cities and never losing a breath. Chuy had wanted Oscar to be an athlete, a vato who had people looking up to him. A man with respect.

Stopping for a break, Chuy and Oscar sat in the living room eating tortillas con jámon. It was noon and the tiles were setting, a few more cuts and they'd be done. Father and son had worked all morning and mostly without talking. Chuy could tell Oscar was nervous about saying the wrong thing, about asking him why he'd went away and if he was ever coming back. Chuy would have tried to answer, but he didn't know why, at least not the kind of why that would make sense.

The woman's name was Yvette, and Chuy had known her from high school. She was still fine, but that's not why Chuy did what he did. Things between him and Teresa were chingada, and in a way Oscar had made them that way—their fighting for who the boy should be was never ending. With Yvette Chuy had wanted another chance, another son. He pictured this boy playing in the park, not thinking about colleges and futures, about all the dumb things he could do to mess his life up. Yvette called Teresa when she'd found out Chuy was married and told her everything.

A car pulled into the driveway, a brown tin can with bubbled tint and smoky exhaust. A man and woman climbed out, some old timers Chuy didn't recognize. They walked with a boy. He was too skinny to be healthy, his shoulders popping out from under his ashy skin, his head swiveling on his neck. Oscar had always been healthy, so healthy Chuy had never noticed. Chuy went to the porch.

"¿Es la casa de Angélica?" The woman asked, her voice tired. The man, who looked even older up close, his hair thin and wispy like a viejo cactus, kept his head down.

"Está adentro, señora," Chuy answered and held

the door. He could tell this was the last chance for them, that they'd tried it all and were ready to leave their hopes to María and the miracle girl. Oscar stood up when María appeared from Angélica's room, like he knew something was about to happen—Oscar had always been good at that. María met the family at the door and was glamorous all over again.

"Ayúdeme con él," the man said to Chuy. Chuy went over to the boy, leaving Oscar alone. Chuy cradled the sick boy in his arms, and even though he was older than Oscar—his eyes yellow and his skin thin and rough—he weighed nothing. Chuy felt responsible for him, like holding on would keep them both from floating away. Oscar eyeballed Chuy—giving him that Teresa look—and he couldn't remember the last time he'd held his son. Chuy wondered if there was something broken inside himself, something jagged. Chuy reached down and tried to grab Oscar's hand, but he pulled away, hiding the taped mess behind his back.

She led everyone to Angélica's room and told them her story. Angélica had been swimming at a city pool when she slipped and hit her head, drowned in front of everybody. At the hospital Angélica was put on machines, and doctors told María her daughter would die as soon as they were turned off. So María prayed for a miracle—Ave Marías, Novenas, everything she could think of—and when the hospital decided to shut her down, because it was too expensive and too late anyways, Angélica kept breathing, living.

María took her to church that day, right to the altar where a Mass was going and a priest giving Communion. She demanded he give to Angélica, and when the cura put the wafer in the frozen girl's mouth, it transformed. The Host softened into a miniature beating heart, a ring of thorns sticking the sides, and it burst as soon as it touched Angélica's dry tongue. From then on María said she could see the Holy Spirit glowing in her daughter's eyes. Angélica had cured the priest's diabetes, or so María had said.

María went on to explain the rules. They could pray and ask Angélica to speak to God. They could light candles and touch her, but only on the arms. No pictures. Donations at the end. Chuy imagined the sick boy touching Angélica and then coming to life, like a dry sponge soaking up water. Maybe that's how it worked, Angélica's body sucking tumors and bad blood and bad hearts and trading it with the life she couldn't use. Chuy hoped Oscar would touch her. Angélica could fix his hand. Fix everything.

The room looked different than it had that first night. The moonlight had been replaced by the sun, making the room warm and inviting. Ceramic statues of San Judas and La Virgen de Guadalupe were in the corners of the room. Prayer candles of every kind of saint—San Cayetano, Agustín, Pascual Bailón, Lorenzo, and Santa Bárbara—flickered and glowed. Angélica lay in the middle of the room, wearing a pink dress with lacy trim. She breathed with the help of a machine, made a slow sucking noise. A purple blanket with small metal hearts and prayer cards, with fading photographs of sick nanas and tatas and niños at hospitals, of families smiling—memories of the good times—and little kid drawings with blue skies and frowning faces were pinned to it and pulled to her waist. The doorbell rang.

Chuy carried the sick boy closer to Angélica. Oscar stayed back. The old man motioned for Chuy to put his son down, and he did, though he'd wanted to hold on longer. Chuy wanted to be part of any miracle Angélica could make. Chuy watched as the mother placed her son's bony hand inside the miracle girl's, could hear Teresa calling for Oscar from the front door. The mother of the sick boy cried, the corners of her mouth lined with spit. María lit incense and made the air thick and cloudy, a bad dream about to end. Chuy knew Teresa would eventually let herself inside the house.

María sprinkled the sick boy with holy water and huddled everyone around Angélica. Chuy grabbed Oscar and took him to her, ready to hope for something, too. They stood next to the sick boy, and Chuy took Oscar's taped hand and placed it on the miracle girl. A layer of black hair covered Angélica's cheeks and above her lip. An oily patch of acne around her nose. Chuy felt pinche for noticing, for butting in, for letting things get bad enough for miracles in the first place.

"Pray," Chuy said to Oscar. Chuy hadn't prayed in years because asking for help had never done him any good, but as he closed his eyes and squeezed Oscar's hand, he surprised himself. He asked for whoever was listening to make things right for the boy. Chuy opened his eyes and turned around, saw Teresa in the doorway.

"Oscar," Teresa said, waving him over.

"Má," Oscar said, suddenly breaking from Chuy and running toward her. Chuy backed away from Angélica. The family hadn't noticed them, like they were all frozen in some terrible painting: the sick boy's parents

23

with heavy heads, María's clenched face, the sick boy and Angélica lost.

Teresa looked over Oscar's hand on the porch. They were out of place by the scraps of tile and empty bags of thinset and grout, the tossed around tools. Teresa peeled off the tape. The kitchen towel was soaked with blood, and the adhesive left a grayish gum on the outside of Oscar's wrist. His hand was still clenched in a fist.

"What happened?" Teresa asked.

"It was my fault," Chuy said, meeting them outside. "A tile cut him when I wasn't looking." Oscar tried to hide his hand, but Teresa grabbed it.

"Look at his hand, Chuy." Drops of blood fell to the ground. "Ábrate la mano, Oscar." Oscar didn't move, and Teresa pulled his fingers open. Clumps of red flour caked the rim of the wound, fresh blood in the middle. It ran down Oscar's arm as Teresa lifted it to show Chuy. It looked worse than before. How could he not have known how bad the injury was, that the boy needed to be looked out for? "This needs a doctor, Chuy. Why didn't you call me?"

"I told him to tough it out," Chuy lied. "That we had a job to finish."

Chuy thought of Angélica, of the small twitching heart pulsing and flexing on the surface of the miracle girl's cracked tongue. Her body would keep living, spreading until her pink dress got too small and she became a burden to anyone who loved her. Chuy didn't know if Angélica had ever cured cancer or anything else. Her life was a silent and stuck way to be. A life Chuy knew.

"I can't believe you," Teresa said, rewrapping Oscar's hand.

Teresa picked up their son. He was too big for her, but she lugged him to her car. Feet dragging on the ground as he slipped from her arms. Teresa belted Oscar in the back seat, looked ahead as she cranked the engine. Oscar turned to look at his father, and Chuy, knowing better than to turn away, waved goodbye.

Airman

Tent City has gone quiet. There is a deadline. I heard it on the news. I've never thought about the word before. How in this place it means what it means.

Dear Linda,

I thought about you on the flight. The plane shook like crazy, and Pandullo puked himself. I remembered you telling me how your baby brother got sick and smelled up the car on summer trips to California. I imagined you rolling down the window and sticking your head out. I pressed my head against my own little window and watched the ocean. That was as close as I've ever been to it, the water moving and me wanting to jump in. Maybe you could take me to the beach where you went swimming, if we ever see each other again.

We landed in the middle of the night. The whole camp is razor wire and watchtowers. We got briefed: no going off base, no booze, no phone calls home for at least a month (you should send me your number). They set us up in Tent City, a group of tan flaps lined in rows. We each got a cot, a pillow, and a blanket, then an A-bag, a C-bag, and a flak vest. I watched the older guys and did what they did, unpacked my duffel and marked the back of my Kevlar helmet with masking tape. No one expects to need chem-gear, but they say the enemy has nerve gas and blood agent and who knows what else. I checked my mask over, just in case.

I slipped pictures in the Velcro seals above my cot. There's one with my má and pops standing next to each other at my cousin's quinceañera—those two don't smile for shit. There's another with Beto and Manny, my older brothers, all drunk and toothy the night before I left for boot camp. Beto's eyes are red from the camera. I hung one with me and Ana. I put it because everyone had more pictures than I did, and I didn't want them knowing I got no one back home. If I had your picture, I'd put it up and take Ana's down like nothing.

Pandullo felt better after landing. He's nineteen like me, except he's already hooked up with a wife and kid. Pretty nuts, huh? He's my three-man. We talked about Country, our ate-up loading chief. On the plane Country had told Pandullo to keep an eye on me, make sure I didn't crack up. He doesn't like Mexicans. Do you get that from people in college?

Country didn't want me on his crew when I first got to base, but I showed him what was up in the load-barn, learning GBU-10s, 12s, 27s, and 87s real quick. I've won Load Animal three times. Being a two-man is about hustle. I walk bombs from the trailer, line them up to the rack and sway them down. I do this faster than anyone. I check out seeker-heads, fuse and wire and cart. I've always been good at turning wrenches. I bought The Motorcycle Diaries, by Enrnesto "Che" Guevara, the same one you were reading, with the coffee ring on the back cover.

I hope you don't mind me writing this, but you were looking good at that bookstore. If I'd known girls as fine as you were hiding inside, I'd have gone in sooner. I only went because I promised má I'd buy a bible before I left. Maybe us meeting is fate, you only in town to see your cousin off and me deploying with him. I didn't even get the bible—can you believe that? I'll keep an eye out for your primo. Joel Guzmán, right?

I'm getting tired. The cot is rough, scratchy green cloth sewn to short aluminum legs. I'm not sure when I'll get the chance to write again. No one knows what our schedule will be, if or when the war starts. Country said nothing's going to happen, "All this just a waste of damn time." I bet he's right.

Sincerely,

Tomás Cota

Dear Linda,

I'm not sure how long the mail is taking, and I hope I got your address right. My folks already sent me a letter. I've read it twice, and I will probably read it again after writing this. They're not doing too good. Tata had a stroke. I'm not sure what that is exactly, but they found him passed out on the porch, a rosario balled in his hands. He's in a coma. Pops wrote that he'd started acting funny, roaming around the house and talking about ghosts, said their faces were hollow. Má told me to pray to San Judas and sleep with the bible under my pillow. Like somehow that will help. Still, I feel bad for not getting one. You had my head wrapped up that day.

Have you started back at school? Maybe one day you could write a story about me, your friend Tomás from the Air Force. You would get an "A" for that one, no doubt. I haven't found your cousin. He's not a flightline guy. I checked. No one seems to know a Joel Guzmán. Where does he work? Does he have a nickname? Country's real name is Barry and we sometimes call Pandullo, "Pandy." I'll keep a look out.

So far all we've done is unpack our toolboxes and wipe down jets. We toured the bomb dump. I've never seen so many munitions. The bombs were stacked one on top of the other and could take up a football field. I ran my hand over one, taking a layer of sand off the body and sharp green fins. I can't imagine loading all these.

I watch the news everyday. I bet you know all about this political stuff. I've never paid attention to all that. They keep talking about weapons and war and show groups of pissed off Hajjis burning the flag. People are getting spooked. The Hajjis that work on base don't look us in the eye and Country says its because they know what's coming. Some of them work in the Chow-Tent, and I had to guard them the other day, make sure they didn't poison the food or put a bomb somewhere. I remember you called TV a "real propaganda machine," and I wondered what you'd meant. You have perfect teeth.

You're not like the girls I know, only caring about landing a man and then being worry free. After high school all Ana wanted to do was get married, move to an apartment and put up curtains while I worked construction with pops. Ana was like that because I took her cherry, but also because she really wanted to be someone's wife, then a mother. I could tell she didn't love me all like she said, and her eyes got big and stupid when I told her I was leaving for the Air Force with no plans of taking her along. I don't want to stay in El Paso forever. I don't want a woman who wants a family more than she wants me.

Have you ever been with a guy like me? What would your college buddies think if they saw us together? Probably wonder why you were killing time with a cholo, a grease monkey GI. Tata once told me, "If you want to be a man you gotta get things done on your own. See the world for yourself and decide what you're going to do about it." That's what Che did. That's what I'm doing.

Tomás Cota

Dear Linda,

I found Joel. I was thinking you didn't have a cousin. Pandullo found him working on the frozen generators behind our tent. It rains hard at night and icicles freeze on the power lines and watchtowers. Pandullo and me throw rocks at them, knock the big ones down and bust the layer of ice on top of the sand. The ground looks like broken glass when were done. I've started Che's diary again.

I work nights and afterward wait outside the Comm-Tent to call home. Most of the time I can't get through, but that's okay. My familia has things to worry about besides me. So I watch the sun rise over the burms and listen in on phone calls home. Country fights with his old lady non-stop; Pandullo does baby talk. I lose track of the days, each one passing like the same no-brain movie they show all day at the Rec-Tent.

Your cousin is an AGE troop. I asked him for your address, to make sure I have the right one, but he didn't know it. He told me you went to school in New Mexico, and I felt better knowing you didn't lie. He said to watch out for you. That you think you're "all-good" and wouldn't write back no matter how many pages I sent you. I wanted to fuck him up for saying that. I told him he had you all wrong, how we sat facing each other on those puffy red chairs at the bookstore, you telling me why war was bad and really wanting me to like you.

Che wrote that during his trip to South America he wanted to help all the poor people he met. Maybe that's why I'm here. I could be as good as that dude. I told Joel you wanted me in that bookstore—I could tell. Joel called you a snob. I don't know why you'd want me to keep a look out on a guy like Joel, but I will.

Pleas write soon,

Tomás

Linda,

I talked to Má on the phone. She's not doing

good. Tata is still in a coma, and now she's been having nightmares. In the dreams she is huddled around a cactus in a backyard, surrounded by people dressed in layers of rotting clothes, protecting themselves from the snow. The sky is gray and freezing. She is sure they are ghosts. Má made me promise to read my bible and pray hard for things to turn right. I went to the Chapel-Tent after we talked, tried to get right with her and God. I found the Base Chaplain. It turns out he had bibles to give, and I took two small ones. I keep one under my pillow and the other in my pocket, that way I can finish reading the whole thing. I've started praying to San Judas and Santo Niño, but I don't know if praying works. It feels like wishing, which never does.

I sometimes close my eyes and try to remember what you look like—Country thinks I'm sleeping on the job. I remember your face, your wide nose and chubby earlobes, your black hair. I don't know why I do this, why you stick in my head so bad. I know I'm making too much of you, but I can't help myself, like if I don't I won't remember who I am when this is over.

Má told me pops spends his days at the hospital, crying for Tata. I've never seen him even look sad, only pissed off. I don't know who else to tell. I don't want people to think I'm losing it or going soft. Your cousin has been avoiding me around camp. Now that I know him, I see him everywhere: the Chow-Tent, the PO-Tent, the Laundry Trailer. Have you told him something about me? I want to go home.

Tomás

Dear Tomás:

Please do not write me again. You sound like a crazy person and have the wrong idea about us, and your letters, the third one especially, were completely inappropriate. We had a nice "talk" at the bookstore (Lloyd's Books, by the way), but that is all. You seemed interested in Che, and I thought you could use some background information before you wasted your money on something you would not understand. I regret giving you my address. I felt sorry for you. You should forget about me and reconsider things with Ana. The way you describe her, she sounds perfect for you.

Also, what you and your "friends" are doing over there is wrong. If I had known what you did specifically, I would not have spoken with you in the first place (At least Joel only fixes heaters). You need to wake up. What you are doing there is nothing like what Che did. He gave up all he had to protect the poor, all his family's wealth. What have you given up? Who are you protecting?

Linda

Linda Guzmán,

You lied in your letter. I can tell when a girl's in to me, and you were. We'd talked the way people do when they'd rather be wrapped around each other instead of only sitting close, with hands touching, the little hairs sticking out. You talked about revolutions and corporations and then stopped and waited to see if I was impressed. We had a dance going. I let you lead.

You can put whatever you want in your letters, but I know what I know.

Che was a soldier, fighting and killing, everything that could happen here. If my parents had had the money, who knows? I could've been smart like him, had the chance to abandon everything instead of hoping to make my own life better. Still, I understand what Che writes and what he means. "The stars drew light across the night sky in that little mountain village, and the silence and the cold made the darkness vanish away. It was as if everything solid melted away into the ether, eliminating all individuality and absorbing us, rigid, into the immense darkness." After reading so much of these words, words I can't put together no matter how hard I try, I know that this is the kind of vato you go for, even when you want one like me.

We've been flying the hell out of our planes. Country thinks the war could kick up any day. He's fighting with his wife. I watched him yell at a letter. She's missed some bills, and his kid got expelled from school. She wants a divorce. I almost feel sorry for him. Pandullo can't get a hold of his wife. He thinks she moved back to New Jersey with her parents, cleaned out their house and turned off her phone, took the kid. He cries at night. I've tried the bible, but the words are hard. I feel stupid and can't get a hold of anyone back home.

Tomás

Linda,

Tata passed (he actually died two weeks ago). Pops wrote that Tata went looking peaceful. He was always like that. I went for a walk at the bomb dump and cried. It looks like a cemetery, each blue bomb body like a tombstone. Má still has the nightmares, only now she thinks they're visions of the end of the world. I wrote back, telling them not to worry about me. That I was fine. I feel bad for always lying to them. The phones have been cut off.

Everything over here is flat, no mountains, no trees or even spiky bushes. No wonder the Hajjis are always pissed; they don't have nothing to block the sun or stop the wind. Everything's always in their face. Tent City has gone quiet. Even Country has shut his mouth. There is a deadline. I heard it on the news. I've never thought about the word before. How in this place it means what it means.

Sincerely,

Tomás

P.S. Maybe I should have stayed with Ana, but I didn't.

Linda,

I was rereading Che's diary when Country burst inside the tent and yelled, "Grab your shit and head to the line. Time to load!"

They bused us to the flightline, the same kind kids ride to school, with the drop-down windows and missing seatbelts. My stomach jumped to my throat and my hands twitched as the bus slipped through the cement barriers. The GBUs had already been delivered. I pushed my toolbox to the flightline and prepped the stations, running through the steps in my head: sensing switch straight, hooks open, ejector feet set, sway arms retracted. Pandullo cranked the jammer and a plume of black smoke stunk up the air, the motor making a wheezing put put put sound. The first bomb was off the trailer before I was ready, and I hurried to wire the BFDs and cart the stations. Sweat dripped off my arms and ran down my legs. My hands smelled like metal. I hadn't been sleeping right, my mind all over the place. Country guided the bomb toward the first station. He yelled, "Hurry the fuck up, Cota."

The first bomb didn't go up pretty. Country struggled to lock it in without tangling the arming wire in the hooks. Pandy had come in crooked. We've done this a hundred times, practicing month after month. Country grunted as I jerked the tail, rolling the 2,000-pound mess into the rack. He locked it in, and I was relieved when I heard the clack of the hooks. I got my rhythm after swaying the first bomb down. Everyone did. The next bomb went up easy, then the one after that easier still, then easier and easier.

I didn't notice the crowd that had gathered to watch. Some bullshit airman like us, pilots and a group of civilians I'd never seen before. After we'd finished, Country took a grease pencil and wrote, "God bless the USA" on the first bomb we loaded. Soon slogans like,

Twitching Heart

This is for 9/11 and Fuck Rag Heads, We Will Never Forget and Greetings from the USA, covered the bomb body. Country handed me a grease pencil and told me to put something down. I'd earned it. I found space where the guidance fins bolted to the explosive body. I wrote my name.

There wasn't a star in the sky—no moon. I'd never seen it like that before, like someone had unplugged outer space. We smoked cigarettes after the launch, my hands shaking. Country looked happy with himself, like if he were to die at that moment it would be fine with him. I thought about his kid, how after getting kicked out of school he wouldn't even have the chance to end up here. Pandullo stayed quiet. We loaded more bombs than any other crew.

Who knows where these bombs are going? The air is hot and I have trouble breathing. There is a radio playing the news, and I hear the voice of a woman talking, but no word of bombs or explosions or numbers of people dead (not yet anyways). There is something heavy in her voice, like after tonight the world will be different, worse than before. I've never thought about the job I do—even while here and after all the times loading I've never really given it much thought. But I am now. I'm thinking pretty hard now.

Tomás Cota

Matt Méndez

Linda,

They called everyone into the hangar hours after the last plane returned, the bomb racks clean. The commander spoke. He said things like "target of opportunity" and "high priority objective." A television had been wheeled in the middle of the hangar. He turned it on, and I watched from behind Pandullo. The TV had a gray sky view of a city block, a crosshair on a stone building that didn't look high priority or like any kind of opportunity I could think of. Just a store in a neighborhood. The hangar was quiet because we knew what was coming. I heard the pilot sucking air through his mask. The crosshair began to shake above the structure, and I wondered what the pilot had been thinking.

The bomb looked like the shadow of a diving bird, and after impact the building ballooned into a cloud of black dust. There was no audio, no ka-boom or sounds of falling rocks. Everyone clapped and cheered, even me. I wanted terrorists, whatever enemy we were fighting, to be in that shop, to make the happy feeling I had easier to like. We were all guilty of wanting to see what a bomb could do.

They showed another, this time a grainy figure running toward the objective, a man not making it inside the small house before impact. They played more, one after the other until I quit counting. I couldn't really think with all the noise. Only about the man and why he was running to the target instead of away. He never got to see what or who was inside the home. Neither did we.

I thought of the first bomb we loaded, my name somewhere on a tiny twist of metal, proof I am part of this. Evidence that Country, Pandullo, and me are in a war, but the war still seems far away watching from a TV screen. In the hangar everyone seems glad it's that way, happy to have no ugly memories so we'll always feel good about bombs and freedom, God blessing America forever.

Country said it wouldn't be long until we head home, a few more days of heavy bombing and the Hajjis would surrender, but Country's wrong. The war has just started and Linda, wars don't ever seem to end. If it were my home being attacked I would never stop fighting. I'd find Ana and make babies to keep the fight going even knowing one day the sky would drop on me, but I'm not on that side. I'm on the side of a country that's more afraid than anything else, and I'll probably be loading bombs until those feelings change. I don't know what comes after fear, just like Che didn't know what came after outrage. Just like you don't know anything about this.

Flores

The wings aren't magnificent, instead bald in spots with patches of pink and blue-green veins webbed underneath the skin.

Flores lies awake on a mattress made of oily blankets and cardboard. Ready for the night to start, he stretches his arms and legs, but the painful knots of muscle never fully untwist, instead squeeze against his bones as he rolls out of bed. The walls of Flores' one room shack are plywood, the floor unfinished concrete. Music pushes through holes in the roof, bass thumping through rusted slats of sheet metal. Causes a rattle that won't stop until hours past sunrise. Whistles and sirens, the sounds of desperate fiesta wait for Flores to join them outside.

Every night in Ciudad Juárez is the same for the old man, him working a Polaroid camera, snapping photos of kissy-face couples and borrachos as they stumble along rows of nightclubs and bars. This has been Flores' job for years, a blur of smiles and flashes for two bucks a shot. But tonight is going to be different, or at least it will be his last. Flores' friend, Uriel, the angel, having promised to kill him by morning.

He puts on his tuxedo, slips on black slacks that are too short, tucks in a ruffled dress shirt and ties a bowtie. His fat knuckled fingers work the strip of cloth into a perfectly flared bow then strain when lacing the creased leather shoes he wears without socks. The tuxedo jacket, thinning and with holes, is like another skin, wrinkled and papery and stinking of cigarette. Flores reaches through the sleeves and digs into the breast pocket, pulls out his fading photo of Monchi, his long ago murdered wife.

The borders are yellow, and Monchi's black hair has turned brown, her toothy smile bleeding into whiteness that spreads across her face. Flores closes his eyes and tries to picture the woman he still loves, but his failing mind plays a trick, only recreating her whitening image. Flores knows the chemicals in the film are dissolving away, and when they do he'll lose Monchi. Her face, his memories, gone for good.

Set to die Flores walks Avenida Juárez for the final time, camera hanging around his neck. The red and blue lights on police trucks flash; street vendors push their carretas across clogged streets, making their way toward the bridge to sell homemade jewelry and candy and bootleg movies to Americans happy to be heading back across. Flores moves past the row of cars inching up the busted asphalt, struggling like blood through a collapsing vein. He wonders how many beats his heart has left.

The bus station is only a few blocks down the street, where Flores has asked the angel to meet him. He picked this spot because the women of the maquiladoras gather here before heading back toward the clubs, them looking to blow off steam after hours behind presses and assembly lines making blue jeans and brake pads and shit that gets used up. These women come to Juárez from all parts of México, searching for some kind of new beginning, but what they get is a city with a past so heavy the future can't get up from underneath it.

The last packet of film snaps inside the camera, and Flores listens to the whirr of the small gears turning inside. A bus arrives, and the women who pour out are dressed to party. They wear miniskirts and tube tops, flowery blouses and jeans with gold embroidery along the legs: ZAC for Zacatecas, COAH for Coahuila, and CHIS for Chiapas. Flores takes a picture. The image of a woman seeps from the blackness of the ejected film. She is young, a girl really, and Flores tries handing her the photo, but she quickly runs from him, slaps the picture from his hand and sends it floating away.

Flores chases after her. Feels the ligaments in his knees ready to snap as he struggles to keep up, insides burning as he reaches for the girl. He wants badly to touch her black hair, bare shoulder or arm. To inhale the perfume he knows she's wearing in small dabs on her neck. Flores tries screaming for her to stop, that he's harmless, but all he does is grunt. A noise that comes from somewhere in his gut, a deep and moaning sound. The girl shrieks, and the women watching from the station scatter and disappear.

Alone in the chase, Flores starts to think it's Monchi who's escaping him. She's gaining speed and distance, moving from the sidewalk and up the middle of Avenida Juárez. She's a shadow in the oncoming headlights. Slow moving beams about to cut her down. Flores keeps pursuing as tires chirp and horns trumpet in a long one-note song. Metal smashes and buckles, but over all the noise Flores swears he hears Monchi in his ear, telling him how sorry she was for having to leave but a baby born dead was too much. A poison field of strawberries no place to live.

That's when Uriel blindsides Flores, knocking him to the ground with a lowered shoulder after appearing from behind a phone booth. Flores cradles his camera as he crashes to the ground, the strap around his neck breaking. Uriel walks toward him, a rusty pipe in his hand. Flores slowly takes his feet, bends at the waist and wheezes, coughs and spits brown snot. He looks up and can't see Monchi, remembers that Monchi is dead and scans for the girl, but she's gone, too. Cars have wrecked to a stop, pissed off vatos standing beside them looking for someone to blame for the pileup.

The angel looks like a skinny teenager, greasy face and slicked back hair. Uriel taps the pipe against the ground. It makes a hollow sound, sheds rusty flakes.

"What the fuck are you doing? You trying to hurt that girl?" Uriel says, grabbing Flores and pulling him out of sight.

"No, only wanted to give her a picture, a good memory. " Flores says, out of breath.

"No way she forgets the sucio who chased her tonight, trust me." Uriel finds a bench and sits. His face looks broken, lips chapped and cracked, dried blood crusted around his nostrils and down his shirt. "Where do you want to do this?"

"Where they found Monchi. Where I put her cross."

Flores slumps down next to him. He's sweating

through his tuxedo. Wet under his arms and down his back. Flores closes his eyes. His shoulder is a mess, elbows and knees soppy with blood, but at least the camera is in one piece. He runs his hands over the lens, the pitted plastic housing and the warmth of the battery.

"Man, why you always chasing after bitches?" Uriel says.

Flores met the angel in a bar, a lonely cantina with no music and black paint on the windows, no daylight allowed. They became drinking buddies, both talking shit after spending the morning drinking cheap tequila and wine. Uriel usually talked bad about La Virgen and San Gabriel Arcángel. Called them both phonies and said anyone wasting time praying to those two scammers would be better off sucking his non-existent cock. Flores didn't have anything against the Blessed Mother or the Archangel, but God was another thing.

Monchi sent Flores a Dear John letter the day she arrived in Juárez, after months of nothing, Flores hoping maybe she had changed her mind but instead warned him not to follow—a mistake he was done making—and wrote that it had been God's will for her to leave and start over. That everything grown in those California fields, not only their baby but also their life together, had been doomed from the beginning. It was clear to her, now. So clear that when Flores later received a second letter, a slim government paragraph explaining how Monchi's body had been found under a stack of tires at the edge of town, he almost couldn't believe it. Flores came to Juárez with his photo and camera hoping to prove she was alive. He stayed in the city after burying her, wanting to see why God thought the murder capital of the world was better for Monchi than he was.

"Can we go now?" Flores asks the angel.

"We can go," Uriel says. "You're getting cold feet. I can tell."

The two buy tickets and get on an empty bus. Flores points the camera out the window and snaps another picture. The image on the photograph is a streak of black. Flores flicks it on an unused seat and thinks about dying, the heavy pipe in Uriel's hand and how it's not only his feet that are getting cold. Flores brings his arms close to his chest to keep them from trembling, to keep Uriel from noticing, but his deception embarrasses him, and he hopes Uriel will say a prayer for him afterward, hopefully one to the scammer Virgen de Guadalupe.

The bus exits the city and makes its way down a dirt road. Flores catches a glimpse of himself in the bus's rearview. The years in the sun have cooked dark spots into his face. His leathery cheeks have deep creases and ridges in them. Flores' nose is a bulb of California cauliflower.

"So why the camera?" Uriel asks. "I know you ain't some kind of artist."

"No. Not an artist."

"And the money's shit."

"Worse than shit."

"Then why?"

Flores sinks into his seat. The fluorescent lights of the cabin buzz as the bus bounces down the road. He can smell the sour sweat of the person who sat in the seat before him, or maybe it is his own stink. Fear now slicking his body. Making him want to puke. "I thought if I could see the city I would learn something about it. Get to see the big picture, but it didn't take long to figure out you can't see shit from behind a lens. It's only a place to hide."

"Fuck, you are an artist," Uriel says. The angel reaches into his dusty army jacket and pulls out a book. He hands it to Flores. "Trade me for your camera. I'll need a place to hide after tonight."

Flores hands Uriel his camera and wonders if the angel knows he was mostly lying. The camera had belonged to Monchi, was meant to take baby pictures but never got used for that. Flores had taken his photo of Monchi with it, had had fun getting her to smile. Flores takes the hardcover from the angel and slips it into the cut lining of his tuxedo jacket.

"You're not even gonna look at it?" Uriel asks.

"I don't have time to read it, do I?"

With the camera in his palm Uriel considers the question, balancing it like his hand is a scale. "I guess not, but I can tell you what it's about."

Flores doesn't care what's inside the book but the angel tells him anyway. Says it's about ghosts, a whole town haunted by them and worse, memories. Goes on and lets Flores know he's lucky his mind's going to hell and too bad he didn't think of giving him the book sooner. "The Mexican who wrote this could've saved you all sorts of trouble. You're better off forgetting everything. Too bad you're too old to know that."

The bus stops, air brakes squeaking and sighing as the mass jumps to a halt. They are in the colonias, the shantytowns that line the border between Juárez and El Paso. There are homes in the distance, made with cardboard and scraps of wood and rubber and other thrown away bits and pieces found in dumps. This is where the women of the maquilas live, where their bodies have been piling up for years. Flores and Uriel get off the bus, and Flores leads the angel to where Monchi's cross is spiked into the desert ground, her name, Ramona "Monchi" Magón, carved across a thin slat of wood. There are rows and rows of pink and white crosses, spreading far. A hard and harvestless field. Like on the bus, Flores and Uriel are alone, the moon hanging big and white in the sky.

"Are you going to do it now?" Flores asks.

"Is that all you want to ask?"

Closing his eyes Flores again tries to remember Monchi, wanting the gears in his head to turn and spit out more than an image, some feeling or memory that will give him a reason to change his mind, but his brain is a scramble, only giving him groves of strawberries and miles of piss stained sidewalk, hazy faces across his viewfinder and the click and purr of a camera.

"I have nothing." Flores says. "I'm already gone."

"Don't you want to know if it will hurt?"

Eyes open, Flores asks, "Is this gonna hurt?"

"Depends," Uriel says.

Uriel retrieves his rusty pipe from inside his jacket, looks it over as he approaches Flores. The two stand chest-to-chest as Uriel raises the pipe over his head. Flores cringes but doesn't move. His body shakes, a cruel tremor, but he holds his ground before the angel.

"Without memories," Flores says. "We are less than ghosts. I bet the man who wrote your book knew that."

The pipe thuds as it hits the ground beside Flores' feet. The angel takes a step back from the old man, strips off his dusty army jacket and bloodied shirt. Uriel's skin is leathery and stretches tight against his ribcage, his body skinny and birdlike. He spreads his wings and the force of air behind them knocks Flores back. The wings aren't magnificent, instead bald in spots with patches of pink and blue-green veins webbed underneath the skin. Uriel's face changes into a viejo's, with deep scars running across his cheeks and over a black socket where his left eye should be. Uriel opens his arms and moves toward Flores.

"Hold on."

Flores wraps his arms around Uriel and buries his face in the angel's chest. Uriel is warm and slick, covered in oil and smelling of wax. Flores feels their bodies move upward. For the first time in a long time Monchi's face becomes clear in his mind, and he swears he feels her hands in his, can remember the way she took his after their first date. They gain speed, and Flores struggles to breathe. He looks at Uriel, the old angel crying with tears dripping from his cheeks and onto Flores. Mixing with his own. With the moon growing beside him Flores feels the air freeze on his skin and inside his belly. Uriel tightens his grip as the tips of his wings catch fire. The feathers singe and crackle as the angel is slowly consumed by the blaze and Flores feels warm, suddenly in an expanse of whiteness.

Matt Méndez

Juan Looking Good

His má bought the clothes on her credit card and paid for his haircut—still close on the sides but longer on top. Juan's tío, Richard, who works for the city and is the kind of Mexican who thinks he isn't, sprung for the lawyer.

Juan puts on his new shiny shoes. He likes them, and when he stands his pant legs cover the thin laces and around the heel. The pants aren't baggy or tight. Not jeans. They are dark grey slacks, sharp and straight. Juan's má ironed his shirt, starched the collar and long sleeves. It smells like lemons. Juan's tucked in, first time since he was a kid making Communion. His má bought the clothes on her credit card and paid for his haircut—still close on the sides but longer on top. Juan's tío, Richard, who works for the city and is the kind of Mexican who thinks he isn't, sprung for the lawyer. Juan checks himself in the mirror, didn't know how good looking good would feel.

His má is worried what the judge will do and decides she'll skip court. Juan ties his tie as she tells him this, knots it so the end hangs just above his belt buckle and then waits outside for Richard to pick him up. It's too hot for a jacket, but Juan wishes it wasn't, wishes his má would've gotten him the blue blazer with the silver buttons. Juan has put his poor má through enough—everyone agrees—but maybe one more thing wouldn't have been too much to ask.

At the courthouse the lawyer instructs Juan to plead guilty; if he does things won't turn out so bad. Richard tells Juan not to be stupid and sign the lawyer's papers, but Juan feels stupid after signing, after landing probation and a fine he can't imagine paying, a dirty record to follow him around. The judge explains how lucky Juan is to have one more chance. Juan's not sure where all his other chances have gone, and on the way home, his arm breezing outside the window of Richard's truck, he thinks maybe chances are like everything else. That some people get a lot, and some don't.

Thinking there's a reason to celebrate Juan's má throws a carne asada. His *tíos* and *tías*, all his primos, come to the house, even his nana in her wheelchair. Juan's friends show, too. His boys slap him on the hand and back. The girls give hugs and tell him how fine he's looking, but Juan's friends want to leave after eating, after taking all the dirty looks his family had for them. They tell Juan to change out of the white-boy clothes. That it's time to really party. "I'm gonna stay in tonight," Juan says while looking down at his shoes. The square toes are as black as the mountains get at night and look just as good with the stars coming out.

The party ends, and everyone heads home. Before leaving Richard reminds Juan that he's done bailing him out, and his nana says to take care of his má because she's looking way too skinny. Later, with his má asleep, Juan locks the doors and goes to his room. He checks himself in the mirror one more time, thinks about changing for sleep but decides to wear his new clothes just a little longer. The phone rings, but he doesn't answer. Juan opens a window and lies down, closes his eyes and kicks off his shoes. The night air is cool and smells like greasy charcoal burning out. A train thunders behind the house, like one does every night, the chugging engines and blaring horns rattling the windows against their frames. Over the years Juan has learned to ignore the commotion but tonight feels the uproar buzzing in his ears and chest. Juan listens as the train slowly pulls away, until the noise becomes a whisper he can barely hear.

All Anything's Worth

Perla knew everything old could be transformed into something new. Anything, no matter how destroyed, could be saved.

Perla was surprised when only two policemen came to investigate the burglary. She'd been hoping for a team of men in blue uniforms dusting for fingerprints, a hard-boiled detective to take charge and find the *cabrones* who broke into her house. Perla studied the shiny badges of the two standing on her porch, read their silver nametags through the screen door. These cops, Anaya and Téllez, weren't the tough guys she watched on TV, more like high schoolers there to sell band candy or magazine subscriptions. Téllez was a porker, had fat cheeks that swallowed his sweaty face. His partner Anaya was the opposite, a skinny-bones with bad skin who probably couldn't overpower even an old woman like Perla. Eyes big and round like an owl's.

Once inside the cops puttered and stalled in the living room, like they were waiting for Perla to bring them drinks or solve the case on her own. The mantle over the fireplace had been knocked to the ground, her collection of commemorative plates and spoons, gifts from Francisco, mementos of the places he'd visited while studying plants, were gone. So were her clocks. There had been one in every room of the house, each

53

set to chime on the hour. Perla liked to listen to them, would often walk from room to room and enjoy the symphony of clashing sounds, her mooing cow in the kitchen and cuckoo chirping down the hallway. Her living room gonging and gonging.

Perla pointed out the broken window, but Téllez ignored her and wandered toward the kitchen. Stepped over the down curtain rods and demolished coffee table like the point-of-entry wasn't worth his time. Perla's sofa had been dumped on its side, crumbs and candy wrappers caked to the underside of the cushions. Gross leftovers from long ago movie nights with her family. Perla imagined the robbers trying to fit the foldout through the front door, too stupid to turn the thing on its side and then giving up, deciding to trash her home instead. Anaya struggled to flip the sofa back on its legs. Brushed off the cushions and offered Perla a seat.

Perla's ankles and knees ached, but she kept her feet. Her joints had become arthritic working at the Por Libra, the secondhand warehouse where she spent thirty years sorting through mountains of used clothes, oily jeans and ever changing t-shirt designs. Old wedding dresses and puked stained baby blankets meant for resale in places poorer than El Paso. The Por Libra was where she'd found most of her clothes and knick-knacks she used to decorate her home. Perla liked getting use from things other people thought were worthless.

Shards of glass were dug into the brown carpet, sharp points peeking through the flattened fibers. Anaya stuck his head through the busted window frame and peeked into the backyard. The house was surrounded by block wall, every window with a mesquite planted near. The bark turning black and flaking off, revealing the white fiber underneath. Perla never liked the trees. They made good shade but the twisted branches always seemed ready to snap and fall at any moment. Perla felt the wind from outside against her face. It was fall, the sun disappearing early but the air still hot like summer.

"Well, you're right, they definitely came inside from here," Anaya said. "I would guess there were a few burglars, more than two. Desperate for cash or maybe teenagers looking to make a mess."

"Is that right?" Perla said. "You must work in the Obvious Crime Unit."

With the sun setting the mountains looked purple with orange light along the tops, and it occurred to Perla that she might never see another El Paso sunset. She'd already called Francisco, even before calling the cops, and told her son about the break-in. He'd sounded more excited than worried, reminding her how he predicted this would happen, an old woman living alone being easy prey. Francisco told Perla not to worry; he would be there by morning to rescue her. Perla didn't argue with her son even though the thought of being rescued seemed ridiculous. No matter how tough her life seemed to get, and it had gotten plenty tough, she had never been a damsel in distress. Though she did have to admit her little barrio was changing for the worse. She blamed the war. It took a lot of good men away—leaving mostly hoodlums behind—and the ones who eventually came back weren't all the way right.

Francisco lived in Arizona with his wife, worked as

a biologist and was studying the life cycle of saguaro cactuses, of all things. He'd been trying to persuade Perla to join him in the Sonoran Desert, tried convincing her that his dry wilderness was much different than her own. That she would fall in love with it like he had. But Perla wasn't about to go loopy for cactus and rock. She was a city girl, born in Sunset Heights and raised in a red brick house overlooking the highway and the smelter where her father worked. The sound of the freeway, breezing traffic that never stopped, used to relax her. She moved to Central after marrying Luis. In a casita near a park and gas station and a bakery. She loved the little luxuries of her city. Poor but proud and plenty of avenues to ride.

The hallway was a mess, holes punched in the walls, floor laminate ripped and covered with bits of plaster. Anaya ran his finger over an old portrait hanging across from where the TV used to be, swiped a layer of dust from the glass. It was an old family photo taken when Perla was a baby, a black-and-white of her seven brothers standing straight and serious, her *apá* in a suit and amá blanketed in a white dress. Nobody smiled. Perla wondered why the burglars had left the portrait behind; maybe somewhere deep in their cowardly bones they had a drop of respect.

"You don't see pictures like that anymore," Téllez said, joining Perla and Anaya in the hallway. "They seem weird, huh?"

"In those days people cared about history, not only about having a good time," Perla said knowing that was the problem with most people.

"I guess. It's just hard to imagine what life was like back then by looking at old-fashioned portraits like this. They seem fake."

"If you looked at the pictures in my house," Anaya joined in, "You'd think all my family ate was birthday cake."

"I'd believe it for this, gordo," Perla said, poking Téllez in the belly. "That pansa's not fake."

Embarrassed, Téllez scribbled in his notepad and retreated down the hallway, suggested Perla bar her windows to protect for next time, burglaries getting bad in her part of town. Perla ignored Téllez trying to scare her and walked Anaya to her bedroom. Inside the shelves had been ripped from the walls. Her wood carved crucifix—Christ's body carefully hand painted, even the bloody wounds—and porcelain San Juan de Bautista with the busted nose were stolen. Perla's record collection and cassette tapes, her Pepe Aguilar and Vicente Fernandez, Jerry Lee Lewis and Johnny Cash, The Beatles and Pink Floyd and Los Lobos were all gone.

"They took my records," Perla said.

"Were they worth anything?" Téllez asked.

"I paid a dollar a pound for them," Perla said. "At the Por Libra."

"Is that all?" Téllez asked. "They could be worth more."

"After awhile that's all anything's worth," Perla said.

Téllez wrote figurines/records in his notebook, underneath mattress/box spring. Perla stood where her mattress used to be, thick dust covering the carpet like fur. Perla's closet had been cleaned out. Her boxes of Francisco's report cards and school awards. Her jewelry. The insides of her dresser drawers had been emptied, a pair of sweatpants and a t-shirt, bras and panties left behind. Perla thought she'd be embarrassed having strangers looking at her underwear but only felt tired.

A dog barked outside. The shout was distant and seemed lost, with fat pauses between each one. Outside porch lights came on. Living and dining rooms glowed from behind curtains, almost dinnertime. That too had been Perla's life once upon a time. After a day of sorting she'd come home and start cooking, Francisco already home from school and keeping busy in the backyard, digging up weeds or planting seeds from the apples and oranges he'd gotten free from school. Back then Luis was still logging hours at Tony Lama, the boot factory, but usually made it home in time to eat. They ate in the kitchen, near the stove to warm tortillas and get juice from the fridge. Her and Luis both happy to listen to Francisco talk about plants, the sun and water and photosynthesis. She guessed a picture from those days wouldn't have been bad to have.

"There's something under your chones," Téllez said, kicking at the pile of underwear. Loosely wrapped in a thin black veil was a book. Her hardcover of Perdro Páramo, by Juan Rulfo. Anaya bent down and freed it from the veil, handed it to Perla. She felt dizzy holding the hardback and asked Anaya to walk her back to the living room, to set up the sofa-bed because the old metal frame was too heavy for her to lift. At least the cops could be good for something.

§§§

That night Perla dreamt she was back working at the Por Libra, sorting through a mountain of ropa usada. Perla emptied the pockets of a pair of blue jeans, like she always had before tossing them into a bin. She sometimes found money or jewelry, an occasional trinket left behind. Perla balled-up the jeans and tossed them into a 100-gallon bin. Her back ached. There was a row of bins, each one labeled with brand names: Levi's and Wranglers and Guess. There were generic labels, too: Pleated Khaki Pants, Long Sleeve Shirts with Collars, Long Sleeve Shirts without Collars, and so on. Even in her dream Perla remembered tossing wads of clothes into containers that changed with time, from Hippie to Yuppie. Pachuco/Bopper to Cholo/Rapper. There were categories for loose buttons and broken zippers found at the bottoms of the clothing piles. The scraps sold to processing plants and made into roof shingles and asphalt. Perla knew everything old could be transformed into something new. Anything, no matter how seemingly destroyed, could be saved.

Now awake and sitting on the sofa bed with a stiff back, feet going numb, Perla had the urge to call The Deacon and demand her salary. That man had caused Perla almost as much grief as Luis, cutting hours without notice or going weeks without paying, always complaining how business was slow and then driving off in his fancy red sports car, but Perla never thought of quitting. In the morning Francisco would come with his truck and pack whatever the burglars hadn't ruined or left behind. Would drive Perla to Arizona and the saguaros.

Perla walked up Piedras Ave., past The House of Pizza and Mission de Guadalupe, the catholic store where she bought her velas. Walked past Gussie's Bakery and hoped to smell pan de huevo baking, but it was still too early for that. She was surprised how quiet the street was, for some reason expecting more noise or commotion. It had been so long since Perla had been out past dark she didn't know what to expect from one o'clock in the morning. The streetlights buzzed overhead, the yellow lights illuminating empty corners and traffic lights changing from red to green with no cars or people needing them to.

Bogart's was near the top of the hill. Perla could see the flat gray paint of the building and the faded silhouette of Humphrey Bogart on the sign above the door. Whenever Perla heard the name of the bar she always imagined men wearing fedoras and women smoking from long cigarette holders. Americanos drinking dry martinis and working hard at being glamorous, but the inside of the bar wasn't anything like Casablanca. Bogart's had dirty red carpet that squished under Perla's feet. The bar's windows, once tinted black, were now purple and bubbled. There were shadowy booths along the back wall of the room, and the dull lighting in the entire bar meant anything could be going on in them.

The place was mostly empty. Perla recognized Israel, the man who used to run a taquería and whose poor son was killed up the street at a liquor store. He nodded at her and looked away, preferring to sit alone at a table with empty beer bottles huddled around him. The few other patrons ignored Perla completely, and she was happy for it, took a seat at the bar.

Bogart's had been Luis' hangout, a place he'd discovered after he and Perla had been married a few years and Francisco still a baby. His place to think, he liked to say. Perla went to Mass at Our Lady of Guadalupe, had sent her son to Austin High and ate at Kiki's, a restaurant right across the street, but she'd never been inside Bogart's. The bar had always been a mystery to her, and she'd promised herself that one day she'd go inside. Get some thinking of her own done.

The bartender walked over to Perla, carrying a glass of water she set in front of the old woman. "Are you looking for someone, señora? Would you like to use the phone?"

"I'd like a tequila," Perla said. "An añejo, a good one." The bartender was a young woman, somewhere in her thirties and pretty, but she dressed plain and wasn't wearing makeup, her long black hair hurriedly curled in a bun. She wore an apron over a loose polo shirt and jeans. She was drowning in her clothes.

"Coming right up," the bartender said. "Didn't mean to offend, señorita."

"Do you dress dumpy so men won't hit on you?" Perla asked. "You seem like you could be good looking." The bartender poured Perla a double and slid the snifter to her.

"You have no problem speaking your mind, do you?"

"That's right," Perla said. She lifted her glass to her nose and breathed in. "Salud." The smell of tequila, the sweetness of the agave, surprised Perla. How pleasant it was. She took a small sip, wetting the tip of her tongue and set her drink on the bar. Perla hadn't had alcohol in years.

"Would you like me to start a tab?"

"I'd like you to answer my question. Why those ugly clothes?"

"I get tired of old pelados staring at my chest. It's not bad tonight, but come Friday, forget it." The bartender said. "I can feel my chichis burning when I get home."

"I bet every man you hand a drink falls in love."

"No. They tip like we're married. So, so much for love."

Both women laughed, and Perla extended her hand. "My name is Perla." They shook hands, and Perla noticed the bartender's hands were smooth but not soft, calloused like her own.

"Teresa."

"My husband used to come here all the time. That is until he left me."

"Is that right?" Teresa stepped away from Perla. "I don't steal husbands if that's why you're here, señora."

"No, no Teresita. I just wanted to see where he used to come. I don't really know why."

"Whatever you say."

Luis had been a soldier in the last year of his enlistment when Perla met him, her in her last of high school. He'd been alone drinking a milkshake at Campus Queen, a burger joint near Fort Bliss. She remembered how good he looked in his pressed greens, a thick man with muscular arms and wide shoulders. A small potbelly only beginning to take shape. There was indio in his face, a beakish nose with sharp cheekbones. Luis had been the only man Perla ever described as pretty. She'd fallen for Luis that day at Campus Queen. She could admit that now. Despite looking guapo, he'd also looked out of place in his crisp uniform, alone drinking and eating with no army buddies around like he'd been misplaced or forgotten. Perla had been the one to approach him, wanting to keep her find for herself. She wondered if Luis had looked the same way while sitting at the bar, like he was still a discarded treasure needing a home even though he already had one.

"So, where did your husband run off to?" Teresa asked. "If you don't mind me asking."

"I don't know," Perla said, still surprised she had no idea where Luis had gone.

"Really?" Teresa asked. "What, like aliens took him? Maybe that sheriff from Arizona?"

"Maybe. The cops are after him," Perla said."

"I'm sorry, Perla. I didn't mean to joke," Teresa said, pouring another tequila.

"It was time to end the marriage anyway. He was a cheater."

"I kicked mine out for the same thing," Teresa said. "He tried to apologize after getting caught, but I knew he'd do it again. Too many men are wanderers." Perla and Teresa emptied their drinks, and Perla felt her chest warm. She liked Teresa, even if she had a big mouth. "I divorced him and now have to work here, my second job, just to afford the rent."

"I never got divorced," Perla said. "My marriage was annulled by the priest my husband attacked while apparently making confession. It was the first thing the priest did when he woke from his coma."

"Ay Dios!" Teresa said. "Why would he attack a priest?"

"I don't know. He just went crazy. He'd been a soldier. In the war. It did something to him. It's not an excuse."

"Well good that he's gone, and good that the pinche church gave you an annulment. They usually want lots of money for that. I tried for one but couldn't afford it."

"I guess I'm lucky," Perla said. The annulment wasn't something Perla had ever wanted or felt lucky about. Perla had stayed with Luis because she thought their marriage remained valuable as long as she held on to it. But that didn't turn out to be true. When Luis attacked the priest, the beating somehow convincing Padre Maldonado to give an annulment, he'd been able to finally toss Perla and their marriage aside like an old rag. There was nothing she could do about it.

"How much for the drinks?" Perla asked, reaching into her purse, the book Pedro Páramo tucked inside.

She'd brought it with her, in case the burglars returned. "I should probably get going."

"We'll let Mr. Bogart worry about the tequila," Teresa said, waving Perla off. She noticed the book in Perla's purse. "What are you reading? I've been trying to read more. So my son will pick up the habit. I want him to go to college. To be smart."

"It's an old book. A ghost story."

"Is it good? Scary?"

"Scary, but not how you think."

Perla had found the book tucked inside the lining of a tuxedo, the jacket in bad shape, buttons gone and the shoulder pads peppered with burn holes. There was dirt inside the pages of the hardback, along with a crumpled Polaroid that had bleached white, but the book had been undamaged, seemed special and Perla wanted to preserve it.

"Why are you carrying it in your purse?"

"My house was broken into today. It was one of the only things left behind."

"What?" Teresa said, cupping her mouth. "I just can't believe all this hard luck you have."

"My son is coming for me in the morning. He's been wanting me to live with him and his wife in Arizona."

"That sounds nice."

"It sounds like a hot place to die."

"Señorita!" Teresa said, laughing. " I guess that means you don't want to go. Why not be happy to get away. After everything you've told me tonight, I can't see a reason for staying."

Outside a car parked in front of Bogart's, its radio thumping loudly. The noise sounded like a violent heartbeat, a brutal repetition that rattled its own metal frame. A machine having a heart attack. When the music stopped, a group of men, all with shaved heads and tattoos, baggy clothes and too much cologne, walked inside the bar. Teresa and Perla eyeballed them as they walked passed the bar and disappeared into the shadowy booths.

"There's no waitress!" Teresa yelled as they walked by.

"Regulars?" Perla asked.

"Never seen these deadheads before in my life." Teresa continued watching until they were out of sight. "Tell me something, Perla. Aren't you glad you won't have to worry about being around men like these anymore?"

Before the burglary Perla had never worried about men like these, and as she watched Teresa looking over her shoulder she realized she still wasn't. Perla pushed Pedro Páramo across the bar. "If your not going to let me pay for my drinks, then let me give you this. It'll make us even." Teresa took the book, thumbed through the pages and stopped, began to read aloud: There is wind and sun, and there are clouds. High above, blue sky, and beyond that there may be songs; perhaps sweeter voices...In a word, hope. There is hope to ease our sorrows.

While Teresa continued to read the driver of the heart attack car suddenly reappeared, spooked both Perla and Teresa and caused Teresa to drop the book onto the bar. The driver already looked drunk, or maybe worse, eyes glassy and red. Perla wondered what was going on in those booths. She imagined the driver and his friends divvying up her record collection and commemorative plates. Banging her spoons together in an attempt to recreate the awful music of the heart attack car.

"Three buckets," the driver said to Teresa.

"Fifteen dollars," Teresa answered. "And no credit cards. Machine's down."

The driver slowly emptied his pockets, slapped his cell phone and loose change on the bar, his car keys. He retrieved wads of cash from his pocket and dropped them in front of Teresa without counting. His pockets were empty and flopped from his pants like the ears of an animal. Teresa slid the driver three metal pails stuffed with bottles of beer and ice.

"Last call is in ten minutes. Better drink up," Teresa told him.

The driver turned to Perla even though she hadn't said a word. He seemed to be trying to make sense of an old woman out of place in a bar or thinking he knew her face. Perla was sure she'd never seen the driver before as she reached out and touched him on the shoulder, surprised by her urge to comfort him. Israel began to snore from his corner table, and the driver seemed to awaken, wiped Perla's hand away and left with his buckets of beer. Perla remembered Francisco was on his way and thought of the highway, how it had relaxed her as a girl. Wondered if Francisco was enjoying the road the way she had.

"To answer your question," Perla said. "'I've never worried about men like him and don't plan on it now."

"You won't have to with your son around."

"No. I've decided against that."

"You're not still planning on living in that house all by yourself? That could be dangerous, not to mention lonely."

"I'm Mexican, mija. We invented solitude, the cure for loneliness. Besides, I won't be living there anymore." Perla retrieved a pen from her purse and reached back across the bar for Pedro Páramo. She wrote her address on the last page and then delicately carved her name across the back cover. Perla admired her handiwork before handing the book back to Teresa. "Tomorrow morning meet Francisco at this address. Tell him the house now belongs to you. I will call him soon."

Perla quickly traded her house keys with those to the driver's car, swiped the forgotten cell phone and left Bogart's without looking back. She didn't remember cranking the engine or how she managed to turn down the stereo. She was too busy admiring the musty smell of old leather and the dim blue lights of the interior, the odometer reading almost one hundred thousand miles. Perla pulled onto the street without an idea of where to go, but the traffic lights were steady green ahead. Perla hadn't driven in years but liked the way the car felt as she gained speed, how it was old but somehow entirely new.

El Terrible

"What I want is for you to understand that you don't get to pick your fights. Get used to them finding you. That's what this is. Life."

"For who?"

"For Mexicans."

Martín listened from his bedroom as his *apá* talked to the television. "What's wrong with these vatos? They want to be poor and with no women and can't fight worth shit. I know plenty of raza on the bus who'd trade places with these spoiled *Gringos*." Martín's old man should've been asleep but was instead watching a movie about a bunch of supposedly grown men who'd formed a support group and beat each other up because they made good money and didn't feel tough about it, them rebelling against fancy furniture and clothes of all things. A few beers and late night TV was usually his old man's remedy for a bad day, the rest of the family off to sleep and him trying to forget whatever tonterías had upset him, but tonight the tonto was Martín, him getting cut from the basketball team. Martín's old man taking the news harder than he was.

Feeling suffocated Martín opened a window, hoping some cool air would ease him to sleep, but it was September, the El Paso night still hot and windy, and he felt no relief. Martín's sheets were sweaty and sticking to him as he got back in bed. He wanted to sleep, to have the day finally be over, and closed his eyes, but his father had another idea and stormed into the room. His old man stood just inside the doorway, a shadow with the flickering light from the TV behind him, making his father seem like a monster just come to life from some makeshift laboratory. He was still wearing his bus driver's uniform, dark Dickies pants and a button-up, his name, José, stitched in cursive over the pocket.

"Oyes, Martín. I know you're awake. On Saturday you're gonna fight The Deacon's kid."

"What you say?" Martín said, hoping he'd misheard.

"I don't want any arguing from you. Cancel your plans for the week."

"Is this because basketball? I told you I don't care."

"I know you don't, and what I tell you about arguing? Now go to sleep. Tomorrow we got work."

He left without another word, and Martín listened as the television clicked off in the living room. Martín shifted in his bed. Headlights from a passing car lit the room, the sound of a squeaky engine going by. Carlos and César, Martín's two little brothers, were now awake and watching to see what, if anything, their older brother would say or do. Martín rolled over and pretended not to notice them fidgeting in their bunk beds. Martín didn't know The Deacon had a son. Wondered what his old man meant by: work.

The next day Martín's *apá* dragged him out of bed at six in the morning, already dressed in gray sweatpants and his old army t-shirt. Martín's father had been in the service before Martín was born and still wore his hair short, shaved everyday and polished his black work boots to a shine. He told Martín they would train in the mornings and work more after school, just being in a fight nothing to feel good about. They walked to the railroad tracks behind the alley. The hot night had cooled into an almost breezy morning and Martín would have enjoyed it if not for the smell of oil and exhaust. His old man stood straight and crossed his right foot over his left, bent over for a stretch. His fingers inches from his toes.

"What are you waiting for?" His father asked. "You have to limber up."

"Is that what you're doing? Do you want me to touch my toes, or should I stop above the ankles like you?"

"I want you to shut-up and stretch. How about that?"

Martín's old man didn't play, his sense of humor somewhere between substitute teacher and fundamentalist asshole. The old man looked out of shape, short and stocky and with a hard round belly, but he easily pulled ahead of Martín as they jogged down the tracks. Martín's chest tightened as he and his father put a mile behind them, and as his old man continued to move steadily forward, Martín lagged behind, began looking over his shoulder and wondered how long it would take to walk back to the house. Martín's body began to ache, but stopping didn't seem to be an option.

He wasn't in the mood for another canned speech from the old man about giving up. Martín closed his eyes and plodded along. Maybe if he tripped and fell, hurt himself just enough, he could get the whole idea of fighting out of his old man's head.

Martín ditched first period when he arrived at school. He was supposed to report to PE after getting cut, the school counselor placing him there with the other rejects, but Martín cruised the hallways instead, peeked inside classrooms at bored looking teachers and students. Martín was a freshman and had only been in school for a month, but already the year seemed lost. Martín bought a Coke and a candy bar, downed them both while still standing by the machines. The early morning run had tired Martín out, his body both hungry and sore, warning him against whatever his father had planned for later. He headed to the football field, decided he'd earned some quiet on the bleachers. Franky, his best friend, had beaten him to the idea, already smoking cigarettes and leaning against the back wall of the stadium, staring into the neighborhood from up high. The houses looked crammed together, most with junk cars parked in front. Martín walked to the top and slapped Franky on the back. Franky had gotten cut, too. He was a good baller—better than Martín—but liked to goof around, missed too many workouts and coach made an example of him. Martín must have been an example of a talentless player. The football team practiced on the field behind them. Coaches yelled and blew whistles and players crashed into each other; the hollow sound of helmets colliding echoed in the stands.

"Didn't feel like hanging with the new PE class?" Franky asked. "You not ready to grow from the experience?"

"Have you and my old man been hanging out?" Martín said. "Making sure I grow up to be some kind of tough guy?"

"Shit, your pussy's more hurt than I thought. The basketball team's gonna suck anyways. Who cares about the team? " Franky flicked his cigarette from the bleachers, the cherry floating down and landing in a dumpster behind the stadium. Stayed burning on a pile of trash. Martín did care about the team, or at least about not being on it. Franky pulled a crumpled pack of cigarettes from his pocket and lit another.

"I got other shit to worry about besides a stupid basketball team," Martín said. Martín and Franky sat, the metal bleachers already hot to the touch. They'd been friends since forever, grew up on the same block, dodged the same cops and cholos and hung out at each other's chantes, though Martín liked it more at Franky's. Martín's old man thought Franky was bad news and gave them a hard time whenever he came by, always putting them to work on the yard or making them pass tools as he worked on his piece-of-shit Duster. "My old man wants me to fight The Deacon's son. Whoever that is."

"That is some shit to worry about," Franky said. "He's the new chingón around here."

"Seriously? I didn't know The Deacon had a kid."

"He lived with his moms in Alamogordo but moved

here to play football. Everyone's already kissing his dick." Franky blew a cloud of smoke as he pointed to the field where the team had lined up to scrimmage. "He's about to throw the ball, the motherfucker with the red shit on his helmet."

The motherfucker's name was Bobby Cruz, and the red sleeve on his helmet meant no one could touch him. He was the quarterback. Bobby Cruz was bigger than the other players—for sure the biggest Mexican Martín had ever seen, probably the baddest, too. He was the only freshman to start varsity, according to Franky. Martín had been like Bobby Cruz in grade school, taller than the other kids, making basketball fun for him, but over time his classmates had grown larger, and he no longer had an easy advantage. Martín watched as Bobby Cruz grunted directions from under center before taking the ball and dropping back to pass. He stood calm in the pocket, looked down the field and chucked the ball fifty yards off his back foot, the tight spiral dropping into a wide-out's hands.

"You think The Deacon's got some other kid? Maybe one with a shorter, fatter baby-mamma?" Martín asked. The Deacon was a big shot in the neighborhood, owner of the Por Libra where he bought and sold secondhand clothes from a warehouse downtown and made enough coin to drive a Corvette and wear ostrich boots. He also volunteered at Our Lady of Guadalupe, tried to make himself a saint by donating worn out clothes he couldn't sell and was at church so often Padre Maldonado had himself nicknamed him The Deacon.

"I bet The Deacon's got tons of kids," Franky said. "Probably has little bastards with all those church ladies," Franky said, " but I'm sure your old man wants Bobby Cruz for you. Maybe he hopes you and him will be best friends after he kicks your ass."

Martín's *apá* was already home when Martín walked through the door. Franky had wanted to come and watch what the old man had planned, but Martín left without him. Martín hoped if he got back early enough he could open a few books and pretend to be busy with school work, get his má on his side and put an end to whatever the old man had cooking, but the house was empty. Even his brothers were gone. "Go change and come to the backyard," Martín's father said from the kitchen. "We got less than a week to be ready."

The old man was never home this early. He'd been driving a city bus for as long as Martín could remember, and Martín knew how much he liked to work. He was the first driver at the station each morning and the last to leave his shift—his bus always clean. Martín's *apá* was crazy about keeping his route on time, never stopped for stragglers running beside the bus and pounding the windows to be let on, said he owed it to the riders who showed on schedule. Was his duty to get them to their stops on time.

"Where's má? Carlos and César?" Martín asked. His father had framed a square section in the backyard with two-by-fours, a small patch of dying grass flattened by the boards. Martín was still dressed in his school clothes, in a one size too small t-shirt and a pair of skinny boy jeans that somehow managed to fit loose.

"I sent them to a movie. We have work to do."

Martín's father laced a pair of black boxing gloves on Martín, cinched them tight. "You're going to mess up your clothes. Those cost money you know."

"What do you know about fighting?" Martín asked, not able to picture the old man beating up anyone but him.

"More than you," he answered. "And you're gonna learn boxing, not fighting like some animal. Like I already told your má, I can't have you grow up chasing your culo and wondering if you're a man or not. You have to learn."

"But Bobby Cruz? Dude hasn't done shit to me," Martín said. Martín knew his *apá* thought he was chiple. He didn't want to work on cars and was proving to be no good at sports; his Spanish sucked. Maybe Franky was right, Martín's old man wanting Bobby Cruz to rub off on him in the worst way.

"It's better like that. Nothing personal."

"That's not a reason. You trying to ruin my life or something?"

"I'm trying to help you. No seas *pendejo*."

"I don't wanna fight anyone." Martín felt like a little boy, his voice becoming high and shaky. "I don't want to get...Beat up."

"Oyes, you're either gonna box him, or me. At least against him you gotta chance."

"If you want me to be like Bobby Cruz, it ain't gonna happen. I don't have that kinda luck."

"What I want is for you to understand that you don't get to pick your fights. Get used to them finding you. That's what this is. Life."

"For who?"

"For Mexicans."

"C'mon *apá*. Maybe when you were a kid. Things are different now. We got a black president."

"Tell that to Arizona." Martín's father slipped a pair of leather pads on his hands.

The old man put Martín in the ring and told him the rules: Hit and don't get hit. Martín had never been in a fight, only whacked Carlos and César when they annoyed him. Martín's *apá* held up the punch mitts and nodded his head. Martín flicked a glove at them like he'd seen characters in video games do, and it surprised him how good hitting felt, the smack of leather and the feeling of his old man's arms being pushed back, but after a few rounds of patty-cake jabs the old man swung his arm and chopped Martín on the head with the punch mitt.

"Look at my shoulders," Martín's *apá* said. "See the blow coming or see stars. Move your head." They worked for five rounds, Martín hitting and getting hit, his old man yelling: "I said move your head. Get on your toes and off your heels. Be slick. Jab, jab, jab. Quit slapping the mitt and punch already. Remember the rules!"

"We need to work your feet," Martín's father said after flooring him. "You move like a tree." Martín dripped sweat, dead grass clinging to his arms as he pushed himself up. Martín had never worked this hard at basketball, felt beaten and rundown and didn't know why his old man was coming off like the viejo from Rocky.

"Can we stop now?" Martín asked. "Please."

"No quitting." Martín's father unlaced his gloves and pulled them off. "You're not giving up. This isn't basketball or skateboarding or guitar or any of the other things you once wanted to do. You're finishing this." Martín squeezed his fists. His hands were soft and wrinkled from being steamed inside the gloves. The sun sank behind the mountain, the sky orange and yellow like an old bruise. Martín's father handed him a leather jump rope. "Let's go."

They went to the alley, under a streetlight as it flickered on. Martín's *apá* stood by the wooden pole stained black with grease. Martín couldn't make out the features of his old man's face under the dim light. This man was a stranger, a father he didn't recognize.

"You gotta give me three rounds," he said. "Catch rhythm and lift your feet. You gotta learn to move through pain." Martín's arms were worthless and his legs still done-in by the morning run, but he started jumping and swinging the rope, not sure what the old man would do if he didn't. The rope slapped the dirt and clouded dust around Martín. "Don't cough. Keep going." Martín could hear his *má* walk inside the house, his brothers being loud, but they were a world away. "Be slick but don't slip. Be on your toes. Have balance. Don't stop. Don't stop. Don't stop."

The next morning Martín only made it a half-mile before he stopped to puke. Every part of him hurt, his muscles like straps tightening over his bones. His stomach knocking worse than a misfiring engine. Martín had had enough, kept his hands on his knees, spat up globs of phlegm. He waited to see if his *apá* would let him off the hook, but his old man grabbed him by the arm and yanked him forward. Told him to quit milking it. Martín felt like a mouse in a shoebox, his old man some demented kid shaking it with him trapped inside. Martín skipped both first and second period, him and Franky wandering off campus to Cakes by Sonny. They ordered cheese fries and smoked cigarettes in a ditch, set fire to dead weeds, dry and twisted stalks crackling black then blowing away.

When Franky asked Martín what his father had had planned for him, Martín lied and said they'd only ran a few more miles. He thought that would kill Franky's interest—Franky had been loving the idea of the fight, wanted to know where and at what time even though Martín himself had no clue—but Franky surprised Martín, said he could go for a run and would meet him at his house when school ended. Maybe shoot hoops after.

At lunchtime Martín and Franky sat in the cafeteria with Lena, Franky's sometimes girlfriend. The day had been almost good until Martín noticed the rally signs and banners all over school, posters of serious looking football players—Bobby Cruz front-and-center—pinned to bulletin boards and hung inside trophy cases. Bobby Cruz's name and jersey number had been painted on long white sheets of paper and taped to the lunchroom tables, slogans like: Panthers Armed and Dangerous and Panthers on Cruz Control written on them.

"Everyone's saying you're gonna fight Bobby Cruz," Lena said to Martín. "That his dad told him the fight was Saturday morning. Bobby said he didn't know who you were but would fuck you up anyways." Lena had gone from looking chola in eighth grade to dressing sexy, everything tight and short except her bleached guera hair.

"Who's saying that?" Martín asked. He looked over at his friend. "Who'd you fucking tell?"

"I didn't say nothing," Franky said. Franky hugged Lena and squeezed her lips shut. "Not even to this cute bitch." Lena pushed Franky away.

"Whatever asshole. Don't lie. You've been acting like you were the one going to fight," Lena said. "Saying how easy it would be for you." Lena leaned over the table and kissed Martín on the cheek. Martín didn't have a girlfriend, his only experience with a girl happening the year before when he made out with Sophia Santos at a party, put his hand up her shirt and made her cry. "But maybe it should be you, Franky. This vato's too fine for fighting."

Franky looked pissed as Lena strutted from the cafeteria. She'd been gaming him since summer, curled up to him when she wanted someone to be close to and pushed him away when he wanted the same thing back.

"Why you always bringing her around?" Martín asked, feeling bad for Franky. "She sucks."

"I know," Franky said, looking suddenly exhausted. "Why else?"

Martín changed into a pair of basketball shorts when he got home from school. The night before he'd thought about telling his old man he was done with training and would fight him instead, but that was before word of the fight spread. Martín knew the verguenza of not fighting would be worse for him than any beating; he wasn't brave enough for that kind of humiliation. It was Thursday and time itself was against him. He looked at his face in the mirror, squeezed his skinny nose and poked his sharp cheekbones. The room was silent with Carlos and César gone, the only good part of his old man's locura. Martín took a deep breath, went to the backyard where Franky and his old man were waiting.

"Where the gloves?" Martín asked.

"No gloves," his *apá* answered. Martín stood in the square with his father, the old man still dressed from work, punch mitts already on his hands. Franky sat on the metal folding chair by the backdoor. He'd waited for Martín like he'd promised, talked about Lena and Bobby Cruz the whole way.

"Everyone at the movies, again?" Martín asked. "At least some people are having a good time around here."

"They're at your nana's. Your má's upset with me. She doesn't understand."

"Her neither?" Martín said. "Where are the stupid gloves?"

"I said no gloves. And watch how you talk. I'm tired of the way you talk."

"I'm gonna get my ass kicked and you're worried about me talking." Martín wanted to pop the old man but instead kept talking. "You got everyone at school talking shit about me. The stupid bus driver's kid thinking he could beat-up Bobby Cruz. I'm a fucking joke now. I'm a bigger joke than you."

Martín's father smacked him on the face with the punch mitt, the force knocking Martín backward. "¿Y qué vas hacer? What you gonna do about it big talker? Let's see."

The old man wanted a fight and Martín wanted to give it to him, make him feel like the clumsy nobody with no chance to win. He crouched down and circled the old man, like he was guarding him on the basketball court. Martín's jaw stung. He hated thinking about how to use his body. During tryouts he had to remind himself to keep his elbow in while shooting and pivot foot down in the post. To have both feet planted when taking a charge. He'd never thought about the mechanics of the game before tryouts, coach reminding him day after day during drills: C'mon Torres, this is the easy part. Do you even want to make this team?

"You won't be able to hit me standing like that," Martín's father said. "That's what you're trying to do, right?" The old man acted like all the other bullies in the neighborhood, cruising in go-nowhere lives and wanting everyone along for the ride. Martín squeezed a fist and hurled a right at his father's head. His arm felt like a rocket, the explosion burning to his hand on its way to the target, but his old man slipped the punch and in one smooth motion clubbed Martín with the punch mitt, this time across the ribs, taking his breath.

"You gotta keep your feet under your shoulders for balance. Too close, no stability. Too far apart, same thing."

Martín's *apá* tossed the punch mitts from the ring and stood with his legs under the width of his shoulders, put his hands up. "With your feet *así*, your reach is longer. You don't wanna be wide and dig in too hard." The old man popped his jab, two lefts like pistons. He moved side-to-side, in-and-out. "You gotta be on the balls of your patas, get fuerza with your right toe and keep weight on the left knee. Flex on it when you jab." Martín's *apá* dipped and slid on the yellow grass. He fired punches with power and speed. "Now run and pick up the mitts and bring them to me. Both of you *cabrones*, on your feet!"

Franky took off, picked up a punch mitt and handed it to Martín's *apá*. Martín did the same. The old man tossed the mitts again and again, told Martín and Franky to go faster each time. To use their legs and move on their toes. Martín and Franky lasted two minutes before they collapsed to the ground. Martín felt the different muscles in his legs burn, his thighs and nalgas, calves ready to snap.

"Who's ready to go a round? If you can punch when you're tired you might win a few fights, if you can still keep moving forward, then you'll always be bad."

Probably feeling confident Franky volunteered to go first, and Martín watched as his old man fitted Franky's head with headgear that had been inside a trash bag in the corner of the yard. The old black Everlast smelled like sweat. Had stains by the temples that looked like blood. Martín's *apá* pulled a pair of gold boxing gloves from the same sack and slipped them on, the color faded and worn around the stuffed thumbs and padded knuckles. "Where are the black ones?" Martín asked, but his old man ignored him. He told Franky to get in the ring and get his hands up, to move around. Franky started bouncing, and like on the basketball court, he seemed to know what to do. He danced like Martín's father, not as smooth, but good enough to make Martín wish he didn't have to go after.

"I don't get gloves?" Franky asked. "I don't want to hit you without gloves. I might jack you up."

"Ayer I told Martín the rules. Hit and don't get hit. Right now work on the second part." Martín's *apá* stepped in the ring with Franky. "Don't worry about punching. Learn to wait."

"To wait? So I can't hit you?" Franky hopped in front of the old man, threw shadow punches and nodded his head like he already had boxing all figured out. "I think I should get the chance to hit back."

"Fine." Martín's old man slapped his gloves together. "Do what you want."

This was bad news. Martín knew that, do what you want, really meant: now you're fucked. Franky darted around, tossed jabs that his father slapped away. This frustrated Franky, and he began throwing wilder punches, but those, too, were swallowed by the old man's gloves. "Are you gonna fight or what?" Franky asked and took a step back, watched as the old man slid in front of him and said nothing. That's when Franky had had enough and looped a hard wide hook, and like the old man had done to Martín, he slipped it. Only this time there wasn't an open punch mitt waiting, instead a fist inside a glove that popped Franky's side and took his legs. Franky fell, first a hard thud on his knees and then a blunt forehead to the ground. He was still for a moment, and then the tears rolled as Franky tried to breathe but couldn't. Tried sucking shallow breaths of air through the wet snot in his nose. "You didn't wait," Martín's old man said. "Next time don't be in such a hurry to get hurt."

Up next Martín made sure to keep away from his *apá*, and the old man explained to Martín how boxing was mixed-up. If you want to move right, use your left foot. Move left, plant on the right. The old man popped two jabs and said boxing was both science and poetry, bitter and sweet at the same time. Martín listened, watched his old man's shoulders and waist to see where a punch might be coming. Two more jabs and a right. Franky sat on the metal folding chair and Martín kept on the balls of his feet, slid instead of hopped to get by his old man. Martín felt good dodging his *apá*'s punches, and he turned to look at Franky, wanted his friend to see him getting the moves down, but Franky was staring at the ground, still sniffling, and when Martín turned his attention back to his father a punch stuck him in the eye, a stiff right that snapped his head back. "That's what happens when you think you're winning. Why don't you ever learn?"

Twitching Heart

Martín stared at his eye in a mirror. A mouse had swollen underneath it, puffy and pink and pressing closed. Carlos and César watched from their beds. They'd gotten home while Martín and Franky finished their last three rounds of jump rope in the alley. Martín's má had gone to check on him and noticed the eye right away, even with only the dingy yellow light to see. She called the old man a bruto and told him Martín wasn't going along with his macho bullshit anymore. Martín could hear them arguing in the next room. His má yelling and the old man keeping calm, trying to explain but having no luck. Martín pressed his ear against the wall and listened.

"What is punching him supposed to teach?" Martín's má asked. "How is that being a man? A Mexican? How is this anything but stupid?"

"It's not just punching. That would be stupid. I want him to get his mind right."

"I should call the cops on you."

"Martín has to learn to do things he doesn't want. That being a man is not going from one hobby to another, one job to another, always quitting and saying he wants something better when what he's really after is something easier. Nothing's easy."

"Punching him in the face seemed easy enough for you, José. Martín gets to be any kind of man he wants. His choice. Not yours."

The door to Martín's parents' room slammed shut. The yelling stopped, and the TV in the living room powered on. Martín turned back to the mirror. He liked the way his eye looked and pressed it again, liking the jabbing pain, too.

"Did *apá* really do that to your eye?" Carlos asked. Carlos and César were twins but not the look alike kind, were in fifth grade and already had more friends than Martín. They claimed to have girlfriends and were on the honor roll. They made everything look effortless, and Martín wondered how wrong it was to be jealous of grade schoolers.

"Yeah," Martín said, again pressing the forming mouse.

"What did you do?" César asked. Carlos and César touched their faces.

"Yeah. What did you say?" Carlos asked. "You're always saying something malcriado."

"I wanted to impress Franky," Martín said, surprised by his words, the truth of them. Martín didn't cry after getting hit, didn't fall or walk away. Instead he moved and slipped the double right his old man had thrown next. Kept his balance and worked.

Martín and Franky walked the track at PE. Martín's body was still sore, but he could tell Franky was in worse shape. He moved like a viejita crossing a street. Franky had stayed for the whole workout, left from the alley after jumping rope without saying another word, and he hadn't said much all morning. Franky was weird about crying and Martín decided not to bring it up, liked that Franky was quiet for once.

"Nice eye," Bobby Cruz said as Martín and Franky came around the track. The football team wore their game jerseys and ran plays in the end zone, last minute prep for the first contest of the year.

"Fuck you," Franky said.

"Tell your nóvia to calm down," Bobby Cruz said. "It's not my fault, ese. Your pops was the one running his trap. I had to promise my jefe to teach him some manners."

"I promised mine the same thing," Martín said, hoping to sound tough but knowing he didn't. The football field had powdery lines painted across it, rows of white hash marks meant to add winners and losers.

"I guess I'm gonna have to give you another one of those." Bobby Cruz pointed at his eye. Martín didn't like his eye anymore. The feeling of satisfaction gone, him left with a bruise that was like a stain on his face.

Martín's má surprised him by picking him up after school. She drove to his nana's and parked on the street, the A.C. out and Martín sweating. His head beginning to ache. Carlos and César sat in the living room and watched TV. Martín could see them from the car. Martín's nana lived close to the school and only a few blocks from his family. Martín didn't move, his má still holding onto the wheel and staring ahead. There were grocery bags stuffed with clothes in the backseat. Clean folded towels. She'd been crying.

"What are we doing here?" Martín asked.

"We are here for now," she said.

"Like living here?"

"Yes, living here."

"I want to go home," Martín said. He wondered how bad things were between his má and old man, if it was good for him to like knowing how far each parent would go for him.

"You're not going anywhere. You're listening to me now."

"What about tomorrow?"

"Mira, you're not fighting. Your father promised to never drag you boys into that world. It doesn't go anywhere."

Martín felt bad for causing his má to cry, and so wanting to make her happy he did what she asked, took his clothes inside and kissed his nana on the cheek without arguing. He went to the backyard and dumped the garbage in the alley. He could see the football stadium from there, the back of the bleachers peeking over the roofs of the houses in the neighborhood. The marching band was warming up for the football game. Bass drums thumped and the pops of snares rattled the air. Martín slid his feet in the dirt, fired two quick jabs and a right cross. He could feel his body growing stronger and quicker as he followed the beat of the music.

Deciding to skip dinner, Martín sat in his tío Chuy's old room, posters of Dallas Cowboys and Los Angeles Dodgers still on the wall. Martín studied their faces. They looked serious throwing the football and swinging bats. Pictures of Chuy in his high school baseball uniform, smiling goofy in picture after picture. Tío Chuy was his má's oldest brother, divorced and without a steady job. Hardly saw his son. Martín's *apá* said his uncle was like a worthless dog, spoiled as a puppy and now only good for eating and shitting.

Martín opened the window. The fluorescent stadium lights glowed, bugs slapping into them. He listened as the band cranked out the school fight song, drums again pounding and horns blasting, the crowd cheering in long waves. A metallic voice mumbled through the air: Touchdown! Number nine, Bobby Cruz! Go Bobby Go! Martín had wanted basketball to give him what Bobby Cruz had, to be the center of attention, to be good at something and call it his own, but he'd only wanted it, the feeling no different than when he wanted a video game or new pair of shoes for his birthday, the desire usually gone after blowing out candles and eating a piece of cake.

"Don't think of the heavy bag as just a bag, but as a man. You gotta stalk him. When he swings away from you, punch. When he swings toward you, move. Circle him. He'll tell you when it's time to throw." Martín looked inside the garage from the alley. Franky wore the black gloves and was pounding away. "Put some ass into your punches." Martín had snuck out the window of Chuy's old room, knowing what he had to do.

When he walked into the garage, Franky slumped tired on the floor. He grabbed the gold gloves from the top of the trash bag. Martín worked the bag, rotated his shoulders and moved his head like his father had been telling Franky. Turn your waist as you punch. Step to the left when you throw a right. Get your right side free to put some power in your punches. Get balance and find rhythm. Martín threw punches to the head and body: crisp jabs and uppercuts, double left hooks and an overhand right that rattled the chains suspending the heavy bag from the ceiling. These punches felt better than before, square and with good balance.

"Not bad," the old man said. "But remember, you're not just punching the bag. You're punching through it. You have to go right through." Martín's father sat on his workbench, the wooden legs ripping from the tabletop. He hadn't shaved, wore a white undershirt that revealed the tattoo on his shoulder—El Terrible—the Old English letters faded and green. "Did your má let you come?"

"No," Martín said, out of breath.

Martín's old man nodded. "You ready for tomorrow?"

"Yeah."

His father called The Deacon from the alley, and Franky untied Martín's gloves, tossed them to the ground. Martín grabbed them and opened the trash bag, looked inside. He found a pair of boxing trunks at the bottom. They were washed but still had bloodstains on the legs and around the thick waistband. A folded newspaper was tucked under them, the pages yellow and wrinkled.

"What's all this?" Franky asked, taking the trunks

and holding them up.

Martín held the sports page, the headline reading: Army Soldier and Local Boxer Loses in Upset! The picture below was a shot of Martín's father sitting in his corner, his young face wrecked and blood dripping from his eye, splattered on his chest. A doctor held his chin and stared into his foggy eyes as a crowd celebrated into some unseen happiness at the edge of the photograph. The caption read: José "El Terrible" Torres fails to answer the final bell, loses bid for USBA crown. Martín's *apá* walked into the garage and stood beside them. He seemed bigger than he ever had.

"What's the USBA?" Martín asked not really caring, instead wanting to know how long his old man had been a fighter and why he had stopped, never talked about it.

"A minor belt. You win the USBA and you get ranked, become a contender," Martín's *apá* said. "You get the chance to do something."

"So what happened?" Franky asked, still holding the trunks. Both Martín and his old man stared at him.

"What always happens," Martín's father said, "when you think you're the biggest and baddest. You get your ass kicked."

"Did you get a rematch?" Martín asked.

The old man sat beside the boys, took the paper from Martín and studied the photo of his younger self. "My enlistment ended a few days after the fight, and I spent a lot of time pretending I got robbed. Making excuses for losing. For leaving the army. I didn't give myself a second chance."

"So how'd you get over it?"

"Yeah," Franky said. "I've been going nuts thinking how I fucked up with basketball."

"I found something else, my job driving the bus," his father said. "I got good at it."

Bobby Cruz stood in the corner across from Martín. He had shiny red boxing gloves taped to his hands, matching trunks and no shirt. Bobby Cruz's father had a stool for him to sit on, a bucket for spit. He barked directions in his ear. Martín remembered how The Deacon talked when he collected money during church fundraisers, how he spoke slick to his má but made loud jokes when his old man dropped what he had in the church collections box: Is that it, José? ¿No Mas? Martín wore his old man's stained trunks and army t-shirt, his hands wrapped and gold gloves tight.

Martín had gotten to San Juan Gym early, his *apá* wanting him to get a feel for the ring, the ropes and corners against his back. He'd unlocked the padlock and pulled the chains through the door handles, the smell of leather and sweat strong as they opened, heavy bags hanging from the ceiling like slabs of meat in a freezer, speed bags and jump ropes and rusted free-weights still. A mural of San Juan wrapped around the wall, his robe blue and flowing into paintings of Salvador Sánchez and Jorge Paez, Diego Corrales and Oscar De La Hoya, Earnie Shavers and Julio César Chávez.

People from school soon slipped through the open doors and huddled around the ring. Martín recognized them—players from the football team and their buddies. Lena and her girlfriends. A few early morning gangsters showed up, too. They wore big sunglasses and baggy jeans, long t-shirts and silver chains around their necks. "Look at these fatsos," Martín's *apá* whispered to Martín. "Vatos trying to look hard while being soft all the way around." Franky stood quietly behind his *apá* in the corner, holding a spit bucket and eyewash. Quiet and focused in way Martín didn't recognize.

He watched as his old man shook hands with The Deacon who'd walked to their corner. "I thought this was supposed to be just the boys?"

"No way José," The Deacon said. "Everyone loves a show. It's fun."

"A show?" Martín's *apá* said and pointed back at the growing crowd. "Why are we making fun for them? All they do is fun."

"You can back out now." The Deacon said, putting his hand on Martín's shoulder. "You were the one who wanted to teach the boy a lesson."

"Martín's already learned what he needed to. I was worried about all these people watching your boy when he learned his."

The Deacon smiled at Martín. "Your jefe's a good man, but I think he's taken too many punches to the head."

The Deacon went back to his son's corner and the

crowd doubled in size and turned rowdy. Martín's father rubbed Vaseline over his son's eyebrows and checked the tape on his gloves. Martín knew the crowd was there to watch him get beat, everyone sure the fight would be quick, everyone but his old man. "This isn't a show, Martín, don't forget. This is a pinche fight."

The bell rang, and the hollow ding sent Martín from his corner. Bobby Cruz hopped around him as they met at the center of the ring, his hands low and by his sides. Martín slid to keep Bobby in front, kept his distance. Sweat beaded on Bobby's forehead as he led with a hard right, barely missing Martín. Martín slid and took a step sideways, back to the ropes. Bobby clomped forward and threw a wide left, missed big as Martín backed against the loose cables and spun himself around, Bobby landing chest first into them. Martín doubled a jab when Bobby turned himself around, knocked the sweat from his face. Martín didn't take his eyes off Bobby, kept his legs under his shoulders and stayed on his toes. His old man yelled for him to hook to the body and then the head, to come back with a right, but Martín was already moving. The muscles under his skin feeling slick and smooth.

Bobby Cruz took the shots and stumbled into the opposite corner. His eyes zipped from place-to-place, distracted, like he wanted to see what his ears were hearing. For Martín the racket of the crowd drifted away, like a radio playing from a passing car, but the noise didn't seem to stop for Bobby Cruz, maybe it never did, because he leaned back and heaved the same wild punch both Martín and Franky had tried against the old man, and like his old man Martín slipped it, had a left to the body wide open but didn't take the shot. Instead stepped back as Bobby recovered. Martín wanted his old man to remember this fight, to take pleasure in the work they'd done because it was the last time he'd step inside a ring. From now on he would learn to be good at the things he wanted.

Bobby Cruz recovered quicker than Martín had expected and stuck a jab against his injured eye, stunning him. Martín covered up, and Bobby Cruz punched his arms and shoulders until it pained Martín to keep the gloves over his face. He dropped his left, and Bobby Cruz planted a right that flattened his nose, flushed blood down Martín's chest and the back of his throat. Bobby Cruz stopped punching and looked to The Deacon, grinning at his dad like he'd scored a touchdown.

Bobby Cruz didn't see Martín already coming back with an overhand right. The punch landed clean on Bobby Cruz's chin as he turned from The Deacon. Martín then swung hard to the body and head. Martín's eye swelled shut and his nose drooled black ooze. He had to suck through his teeth to breathe but his legs and fists didn't stop. Martín stepped forward, could hear his old man yelling: "Punch through! Punch through!"

Tacos Aztecas

Israel took pictures of his nephews looking tough for the camera, of his compadres sipping beers and grinning wide. He watched them all in the viewfinder and wondered what each could be hiding.

Israel drove to the church where he planned to tell Cristina everything, but first he needed roses. Israel pulled onto the lot where he used to park Tacos Aztecas, his taquería, and where there was now a viejo selling flowers from the back of a van. Red roses were Cristina's favorites, or they'd used to be. Cristina had changed in the past year, became almost mute after finding Artemio left for dead behind Ben's Grocery. It was Holy Saturday, and Israel knew Cristina would be at Our Lady of Guadalupe, sitting in the plaza. He'd stood her up the night before and church was her place to think. He'd found her there after Artemio, face swollen from crying and sleeping on the concrete steps. Israel knelt over a bucket of roses, the red bulbs closed and petals wrinkled, loose. He cupped his hands and breathed.

"How much for a dozen?" Israel asked.

"Doce, señor."

The morning was young but already hot. Spring in El Paso was not really spring at all, more a steady hot wind and without clouds in the sky. Too much sun and no chance of rain. Israel didn't recognize the flower guy, an indio with a fat nose and ears too big for his head, but something about his demeanor was familiar, calmado and not thinking too hard. Israel missed the sounds of his former street corner, kids playing and dogs barking, parents talking over mariachi tunes. He missed the mountains before sunset, the way hard dirt and rocks and weeds with thorns as sharp as nails were packed together in some whacked-out creation. Israel hoped the flowers would make Cristina miss things, too. She probably thought Israel didn't love her anymore, but that wasn't true. He just didn't remember how to show her.

Artemio's death was Israel's fault, him never learning to accept things the way the were. Israel had been the one who told Artemio to face the boys giving him trouble, to fight back, knowing Artemio had no real chance to win. Israel had wanted his son to change his mind about being a sissy. Hoped a few hard knocks would do the trick, but it was Israel that learned the hardest way possible that his son had never been the one with the problem. Israel guessed this was how life went—everyone alone with the messes they made, no real way to clean them up—at least until Cristina had come to him explaining the manda she'd made.

At first Israel liked the idea of the manda, forgive and forget, and he'd thought he could handle it when he promised to go along. Maybe this really could be a way to start over, but even as he tried to convince himself Cristina's promise of penance could fix everything, he knew it wouldn't. There was nothing about lent or prayer or church that was meant to take guilt away. Guilt was

God's business, and so Israel ended up at Bogart's on the one-year anniversary and got drunk while Cristina sat alone in church surrounded by ceramic angels and saints.

Israel paid for the roses and walked back to his truck. They made him feel good but only for a moment. Inside the cabin the smell of loose tools and sweat soaked upholstery reminded him of his jale hanging drywall and picking up extra cash as a shade-tree mechanic. Israel had decided to park Tacos Aztecas a week after Artemio's funeral, the thought of again cooking feeling wrong to him.

§§§

The Matachines danced, and Cristina watched as they practiced "La Gloria," a dance they performed the last night of Lent, a welcome song for Easter. The Matachines stomped and slid to the thump of a drum and a pair of violins whistling back and forth. They didn't notice Cristina, and Cristina didn't care that they weren't dressed in their ceremonial vests or skirts. Weren't wearing coronas or bandanas with mirrors and medallas pinned to them. Cristina tried hard not to think about Israel.

Cristina had found the Matachines practicing on Holy Saturday the year before, her waking to them after spending the night locked outside the doors of the church. The Matachines were teenagers around Artemio's age, some girls but mostly boys. At first Cristina hadn't been able to look at them, but it didn't take long for their music and dancing to speak to her. Music had always been an easy language for Cristina, one she spoke fluently with her body, arms and feet always keeping nice, hips saying everything loud. The Matachines twisted and turned, young muscles flexing and moving with power, feet pounding the ground. The Matachines were the soldiers of La Virgen de Guadalupe, and they were her vision. She understood then that she needed to be a Matachin for her son. That she should have been while he was alive.

The manda was supposed to end with her and Israel sitting along the back wall of the church, if not ready to start again then at least together in the same room. When Cristina had made up her mind to spend lent praying Novenas and Santo Rosarios, to make confession every week and bring ofrendas (mostly flowers from the señor on Israel's old corner) to La Virgen's nicho, to repent for her sins against Artemio she never thought her life could end up lonelier when the manda was over.

The Matachines finished dancing and soon Cristina was alone. Wind blew through the courtyard, dirt and sand pitting against the stained glass windows of the church. Our Lady of Guadalupe had always been a big comfort in Cristina's life. As a little girl she played hide-and-seek and jumped rope in the plaza only to later fall asleep in the empty pews, her amá all sangrona over it, but Cristina felt relaxed surrounded by the santos and the viejitas who lit candles in the middle of the day.

Our Lady of Guadalupe was where she danced with Kiki Borjas—the first boy she kissed for real—during her quinceañera and where she married Israel while hiding her pregnancy. Cristina stood by the statue of La Virgen, the paint peeled around her cheeks. Blue gown faded a bone white. But now the peace Cristina had always felt in church was gone, and this hurt her almost as bad as losing her son and now husband.

Instead of religion Israel found comfort in food. The way Israel mixed random ingredients to make comida—gorditas de pollo asado, salchichas fritas, and her favorite, Tacos Aztecas (pulled-pork tacos with chopped radish, onion, and jalapeño that were so messy they dripped down her arms when she ate them)—was the way he lived his life. Without a recipe. On their first anniversary he bought Cristina a rotted wooden boat and put it on blocks in the backyard. I'm gonna get this thing going and take you around the world. The tonto had never seen the ocean. And on the night when they were first together, parked and looking out at the sky over Juárez, Israel said to her: Let's make a thousand babies.

Cristina walked to the back of the plaza and stared at the nearby houses with their sagging porches and flat yards. She'd lived her entire life in this neighborhood and never thought of leaving, but the barrio depressed her now, the trash in the streets and graffiti on walls with lettering curved into doomed mazes; even the pigeons that sat on windowsills made her want to escape.

That's when Cristina saw Israel's truck creeping up the hill, toward her and the church. The sight of Israel surprised her. Cristina had imagined Israel waking up in the backyard, still drunk or messing around under the hood of some junker—not giving her a second thought. But there he was. Cristina decided then if Israel came to her in the plaza, she'd go for a ride in his truck. Drive, she'd tell him, drive a thousand miles from here.

§§§

Cristina took the flowers and climbed in Israel's truck without a word, causing Israel to lose his nerve. Instead of apologizing like he'd planned Israel drove home in silence. He examined the little brick houses of their neighborhood with their neat yards. This place could still be right for a family. Israel pictured kids running through the yards with footballs and bicycles and Barbie dolls. He wanted another chance. To make Cristina's dream of a big family come true.

He didn't think it would be too hard, not this time. He'd seen abuelo looking couples (older than him and Cristina, for sure) on TV starting families like nothing, women going to doctors and having babies planted inside them. This had to be something he and Cristina could do. Israel could convince Cristina to go along, give her the life she'd always wanted, that she deserved, but he knew he'd have to come clean about Artemio first.

Israel wanted to tell Cristina his plans in the backyard, and if Cristina decided she was through with him and decided to leave then at least he wouldn't have to see her walk out the front door. He would pretend she was only going back inside the house where he'd pretend she'd always be. Israel looked at Cristina through the reflection in the truck's passenger window. She held the flowers to her chest.

When Israel and Cristina had first started dating, he'd always buy her red roses. They made her smile, even though she knew how corny he was being, him saying: una rosa para mi hermosa; she couldn't help herself. Israel had always been good with girls—not a player but a dude with pegué—and Cristina ended up spending her nights parked on Scenic Drive. They watched the whole city, the rows of headlights cruising the highways, the El Paso lights bright and Juárez dark—the colonias put to bed but awake like always. They made out and had dreamy teenager talk. Cristina wanted a big family with a house and a yard and a dumb dog. Israel would tell her how he planned to become rich, the plans always changing but somehow they all seemed real. Israel and Cristina didn't have a past, only silly ideas of the future, but that changed the night they got serious.

Israel had picked Cristina up that night, had gone inside the house to meet her jefes for the first time. Israel stood in the living room, Cristina's amá and *apá* watching him like a leaky faucet. A mesquite cross hung over a mantle loaded with family pictures. Cristina at her quinceañera, smiling with some dude Israel didn't know but would ask about later. Her little brothers and sisters looked goofy in picture after picture. Grandparents out of place at a Chucky Cheese. Cristina's parents wouldn't let her have a boyfriend, said she wasn't ready for that kind of trouble, but Cristina had wanted to be brave.

Cristina's old man was the quiet type, but the señora made up for his silence, peppered Israel with questions: Who are your parents? Where do they work, and how come we don't see you at Mass? Did you even do Confirmation, y qué quieres con Cristina? Israel answered her. Librado and Elodia Anaya, both with jales at the boot factory (má up front with the phones and pops in the back on the forklift). Yes, he was confirmed, but no, he didn't do too much church. His last answer, a thought he'd had once but never held on to, surprised him. I want to teach your daughter to cook.

The señora led him to the kitchen and told him to make the old man his champurrado—a chocolate atole he drank every night after dinner. Let's see if you're a teacher or a liar. With the ingredients in front of him, Israel got busy. He mixed the masa with water and simmered it on the stove, adding splashes of milk and chocolate and clumps of piloncillo; he made sure to get the ingredients smooth before straining the drink into the old man's cup. Sprinkled canela on top for looks. Israel had done this before—as a chamaco with his nana, at Christmas time—but never with an audience watching, la señora waiting to see if he'd mess up, Cristina worrying he would. Israel liked how at that moment everything depended on food.

Cristina didn't say much later that night; only that watching him win over the two old grouches with one atole made her love him like crazy. Israel loved her too, said so over as Cristina gave herself to him.

§§§

Israel parked on the street. The house needed paint, yard to be weeded and cleared. Tacos Aztecas was parked in the driveway covered in dust and bird shit. He could always sell the taquería—get extra cash for doctors if things went right. Israel jumped from the truck and went to let Cristina out. The wind blew. Israel walked Cristina up the stairs, and Israel didn't know if her holding him was good or bad. She'd let him lead at Artemio's funeral only to later pull away. He didn't blame her. Cristina slipped her arm from Israel's as they reached the front door and disappeared into the kitchen.

Israel stayed on the porch. Inside cabinets opened and slammed shut. He would wait for her to leave the kitchen, didn't want to feel like a ghost haunting his old space. Cristina now cooked all the meals—they never ate together—and never asked Israel to make chile colorado over diced beef, or albóndigas with fresh ground pork, her favorite. The wind kicked up and made dust devils. Israel couldn't believe Artemio been gone a year, how much he missed his boy.

§§§

A vase slipped through Cristina's hands and shattered on the ground. Shards of broken glass scattering across the kitchen floor. The roses had surprised Cristina, reignited feelings she'd thought were lost the night before. Israel had shaved and combed his hair, and she didn't recognize him looking handsome. Cristina didn't tell Israel to drive anywhere like she had planned as she climbed in his truck, instead hoping he'd surprise her. She'd imagined stopping by their old hang-outs in Juárez before heading someplace new, maybe cruise all the way to México City where they'd get lost in a tormenta of people. They could eat and dance and maybe stop at the Basilica to pray, but Cristina knew she was being foolish, and her excitement wilted as Israel pulled from the church and drove through their neighborhood.

Cristina dropped the roses in the sink and began gathering the broken glass. The kitchen counter above her was lined with white veladoras, some burning, some burned-out. Pictures of Artemio taped to each one. Cristina had always wanted a big family but more children never came. Cristina had four brothers and three sisters, all with four and five kids of their own. Her *tíos* and *tías* were worse, made so many cousins she couldn't remember all their names or where some even lived. It seemed right to want the same, but Cristina had been cursed, had heard about it—La pobre with only one—at every birthday party and cookout, but now, with pictures of Artemio looking down at her, the life she never had seemed small compared to the one she'd lost.

Who knew how life was supposed to be? Cristina didn't, if it was even meant to be anything. Growing up Cristina had never been a type, not the loud Chicana who got in peoples faces and made so much noise about La Raza; she wasn't the badass chola throwing down or the stuffy church girl—not yet, anyway. Cristina had only wanted to dance, to eat and be around the people she liked most.

When Cristina had first learned she was pregnant, she'd thought it would be hard getting Israel to be serious about a family. If Cristina was the kind who didn't know who she was supposed to be, Israel was the opposite, thought he could be everything. Israel chased after dreams, and his chasing made him leave the things he already had behind. When Cristina first met Israel he'd been on the high school football team (he was good at catching and not getting tackled), but he quit to take a job fixing up old cars at Galvan's Auto, thought making lowriders would be his ticket. Then Israel stopped doing that to work with a carpenter, planned to build dream houses for rich people and get himself loaded, too. So when Cristina told Israel about the baby—them checking out the Westside and the fancy houses lined with palm trees and bright stucco walls, the windows rolled down to smell the grass—and he smiled big at her, said he hoped the baby was a boy, Cristina knew that wherever Israel ran she'd be running too.

After telling Israel, Cristina was ready to tell everyone, thought her family would be happy and give big abrazos, but her amá put a stop to that kind of thinking. The baby needed to be kept secret, and she had to get married before getting too big. It's the only way, her amá had said, to keep from embarrassing the family. You don't want to end up like La Llorona. Cursed. Shamed. Alone.

But after Artemio was born everything fell into place, and Cristina didn't worry about curses. She and Israel got an apartment. Israel landed a job as a prep-cook at a steakhouse, and Cristina found her place as a mother. Cristina and Israel decided to go for the big family after only eight months, and they tried for over a year, but nothing happened. Cristina read books, drank her amá's atoles. Prayed to San Antonio de Padova. Cristina remembered her mother's talk about curses and became nervous. She watched as Artemio grew and Israel began to chase another dream. Said goodbye to a big family and hello to food. Israel quit his job and spent the money she'd been saving for the new baby to buy Tacos Aztecas. He told Cristina they had time, they'd keep trying for babies, but she knew better.

Cristina screamed as a piece of broken glass pierced her finger. Israel rushed into the room and stood Cristina up, took her to the sink. Blood dripped onto the floor, leaving a trail. Israel opened the faucet, the water stinging as he washed Cristina's hand. Israel squeezed down with his thumbs. Fingernails yellow and cracked. After Artemio died, Israel quit cooking and took a job hanging drywall. Became a drunk. Israel slept in the backyard most nights, and Cristina would often watch as he climbed into the cabin of whatever car he was working on and passed out.

"It doesn't look deep," Israel said, holding Cristina's hand close to his face.

Cristina looked in the sink. The rose buds had come apart, loose petals clinging to the wet metal, absorbing drops of blood. Israel stayed motionless behind her. Despite throwing himself into food, Israel had remained a good father to Artemio, took him to work at Tacos Aztecas and let him be first to try new recipes. Cristina could now say those were the happiest times of her life, but those days ended after Israel found Artemio with a boy from his Catechism class, after Cristina had told Artemio to pretend it had never happened.

§§§

Israel left Cristina by the sink and walked over to the kitchen table. There was an altar where Artemio used to sit—more burning prayer candles surrounded a statue of La Virgen and another photo of Artemio taped above an empty brass plate. Israel sat and wondered how long the shrine had been there, how much time Cristina spent sitting alone with images of Artemio surrounding her. Israel remembered the photograph.

He'd taken it at Artemio's birthday party, the day he found him and Pablito in the backyard, mouths open and pressed together. When he told Cristina what he'd seen while preparing his grill she said he must've seen wrong. To leave the boys alone. They were friends and that was all. Israel knew Cristina was lying and took the camera she normally used at family parties and began snapping pictures. He got one of the suegros sitting uncomfortably on the couch, the TV glowing beside them. Israel took pictures of his nephews looking tough for the camera, of his compadres sipping beers and grinning wide. He watched them all in the viewfinder and wondered what each could be hiding.

Israel returned to the backyard to cook and found Artemio and Pablito still together. Soon everyone would know about his son; Cristina's family, who already felt sorry for them, would get mean and start whispering behind his back. How about a picture? Artemio asked as Israel tried walking by without a word. Artemio was smiling, not knowing he'd been seen. Pablito inched closer to Artemio and tried hard to look like just a friend. Israel zoomed tight on Artemio's face and clicked.

Artemio was killed three months later on Good Friday. It had been a slow day at Tacos Aztecas, gave Israel time to work with his recipe for tacos de mole poblano. He'd been messing with different combinations of chiles for weeks but couldn't figure them out. Taste had gone missing, and having Artemio working close clouded his head. He started sending the boy home early. Israel wanted to quit thinking and mix things up like he always had.

Israel grabbed a handful of chiles pasillas, guajillos, anchos, and mulatos. He deveined and fried them with the bananas he'd brought for lunch. The taquería filled with good smelling steam, but it was missing almonds and garlic. He chopped nuts and pounded cloves, scraped them across the grill. Feeling good about the smell and look of the browning garlic, he dropped everything into a pot of Chocolate Abuelita. The mole would take hours to turn brownish red and have the right flavors to serve with shredded chicken inside a lightly fried tortilla.

Across the street Pablito ran toward Tacos Aztecas, his bony legs jerking like a strange bird's. Israel knew immediately something bad had happened. The day before Artemio and Pablito had been chased from Ben's Grocery by some wannabes who hung out in front and looked to make trouble. Israel knew their type, standing tall but always too much talk. Don't let yourselves, Israel had told them when they came to Tacos Aztecas looking to hide. Be men and go back. Show those *cabrones* you ain't scared. It was the same thing Israel would've told Artemio no matter how the boy had turned out, but Israel didn't stop talking. He told Artemio not to be a mama's boy, that the next day he better go back and quit being such a faggot. Israel remembered Artemio's face, hurt but not surprised.

Israel met Pablito on the sidewalk, told Israel what had happened. Pablito and Artemio had gone back to Ben's, and at first things had been okay, the wannabes only watching through the corners of their eyes. It wasn't until Artemio and Pablito left the store and turned to walk home that trouble followed. The wannabes surrounded them behind the grocery store. They taunted the boys, told Artemio and Pablito that they weren't wanted in the neighborhood, if they were seen again they would get what was coming to them, but Artemio didn't leave, not even when he saw the knife.

Cristina sat with Israel. She lifted up the statue of La Virgen, underneath the Host, a dehydrated two-inch wafer of wheat-flour, salt, and baking powder. Blood soaked through a towel Cristina had wrapped around her hand. She put the Host on the offering plate. Israel leaned back and looked at his wife, face skinny, bony shoulders and arms. They were both too worn down for more kids, no doctor was going to change that, but Israel couldn't go back to hiding in the yard either and finally told Cristina what he'd done.

§§§

Israel's eyes were closed, the wrinkles around them deep. He said he was sorry for skipping out on her, for the cars in the backyard, for drinking too much—even for the boat. Israel told her what he'd said to Artemio, but Cristina already knew, Artemio telling her everything his father had said. And Cristina knew she'd done no better than Israel, telling Artemio to hide himself from his father. To keep from embarrassing the family. So he wouldn't end up alone.

Cristina had been on her way to get milk when she found Artemio. Ben's Grocery was up the street from their house—she still walked passed on her way to church. The mercado used to sell fresh vegetables and bread but overtime replaced most of its food with booze. Cristina didn't have to get close to the body to know it was her son, immediately thought how lonely he looked on the ground and ran to him.

He died in the hospital. There were no chairs in the ICU. Cristina stood and watched doctors and nurses float from patient to patient. The whiteness of the room hurting her eyes. Later a nurse hugged her and asked if there was someone they could call. She spent time with the police. They put Cristina in a waiting room with a television and a hard sofa. Cristina waited two hours for Israel before deciding to take the bus to Our Lady of Guadalupe, the only place she could think to go.

Cristina rubbed the Host with her good fingers, the flat surface smooth and the edge sharp from being pressed under the statue. She'd cupped it in her hands after communion the week before Artemio's Anniversary Mass. It was meant as a final offering for La Virgen because she too knew what it was like to have a misunderstood son. The afternoon light faded and blued the room; the glow of prayer candles the only light. Cristina's finger throbbed. She couldn't make out Israel's face, only the picture of Artemio. When Cristina had been near Artemio's age she'd made love with Israel, and on her wedding day she'd been ashamed of the love hiding in her belly. Cristina had been afraid of what her family would think, afraid to be who she was. She was glad Artemio had never been.

"I told Artemio to pretend nothing had happened," Cristina said as Israel finished his confession. "To deny who he was. I thought the manda would help make my sin right."

"I'm sorry," Israel said. "It was wrong what I did. To both of you."

"Both of us were."

Cristina put the Host on the offering plate. The manda was over. Israel paused for a moment and then returned to the sink. Cristina thought he was going to recede into the backyard, but he came back with a handful of wet petals and sprinkled them onto the offering plate.

"One more gift," Israel said. The Host absorbed the drops of water left by the petals and spread across the plate, expanded from a hard white disk into a soft pinkish flesh.

§§§

The Matachines danced as Easter approached, dressed in red skirts and embroidered vests with wooden reeds that clacked as they moved. The Matachines passed in front of Israel and Cristina, bandannas red and green, coronas reaching into the air like outstretched arms. Israel and Cristina had come to eat and shared tacos de carne asada with pico de gallo. Cristina picked from the plate with her good hand. Israel held it for her. The bass drum pounded between the plaza walls and violins whistled. The Matachines hoisted a banner of La Virgen de Guadalupe over their heads, the plaza loud with gritos and everyone happy the season of fasting was over.

A Girl More Still

Tungi tells Lena to dig in, not to be shy because with looks like hers she don't need to worry about nothing, but Lena worries all the time.

I dream I am a mountain. Alone until the sun dips behind me and everyone says how good we go together. I want to believe, but when I wake up he's glowing outside my window, not wanting company. Lena stops scribbling and rips the page from her notebook, folds and stuffs it in her pocket. Lena has been writing since she was little, practiced cursive and loved making loops, but now it's more than letters strung together. Her words mean something, though she doesn't know what. Unsure Lena hides what she writes in the back of dresser drawers and behind mirrors, stuffs poems between the yellow pages of her mammá's bible.

Lena is waiting for Tungi and their date, told the chubby vato to park on the street and honk. Lena wants Tungi to see her run from the house, let him peep her as she strides toward him. This way Tungi will remember the night how he wishes, can tell his boys whatever makes him happy: Dude, she couldn't wait to get with me, or, if Tungi turns out dreamy, Man, it was like I was there to save her or something. At school people call Lena a slut, which is not as bad as the shit they say about her mammá and brother, Octavio. Lena tries to ignore the chisme, but it's hard. The talk a constant drip in her head.

A horn beeps and Lena runs. Outside the stars are scattered across the sky like spilled salt. The moon a dinner plate licked clean. Lena jumps in Tungi's ride, a busted Cutlass with chrome wheels and booming stereo. She hugs him, presses her chichis against his. He's wearing too much cologne, but Lena's glad he's trying. Tungi drives to Papa Burger where Lena will order a double with fries and a strawberry shake. Tungi cruises Fort Blvd past Delicious and Marie's, Carol's Bakery and Peking Garden. All places Lena goes on dates, where she eats until her stomach hurts.

Tungi holds the door at Papa's and walks Lena to a booth. Tungi tells Lena to get whatever she's hungry for. He's a big boy, not muscles big but fat, and barely fits between the table and cracked vinyl seat. Lena can see rolls of skin stacked like doughnuts underneath his white t-shirt. Sweat under his arms. Tungi eyeballs Lena, not hungry for food but sex. He's picturing the things he's heard about her and wants her body—all the boys who take Lena out do—but what Tungi doesn't know is that Lena wants his body, to become wide and squishy like Tungi and not trapped by her looks. The right curves at the wrong time, her mammá once said while pointing at her nalgas, telling Lena it would doom her into marrying early and divorcing late.

Respect is what it's all about. Tungi tells Lena this; that she's down because of Octavio. This surprises her. Lena's a lot of things but doesn't want down to be one of them. She smiles at Tungi, calls him crazy and orders when the waitress comes. I'm Your Puppet by James and Bobby Purify floats from a jukebox. It's a stupid oldie that cholos can't resist because to them everything's "whatever, well" or "fuck-it, ese." Pull them little strings and I'll sing you a song, Make me do right or make me do wrong. Tungi asks what Lena remembers about her carnal, that they were only kids when he got put away, all because of that faggot. Lena doesn't remember much. She's read Octavio's prison file online: height, weight, and race, how he fatally stabbed Artemio Anaya behind Ben's Grocery and fled the scene. He looks lost in his death row photo, shaved head and open mouthed, eyes like wet rocks. Lena squeezes Tungi's hand and tells him Ocatavio is dead even though he isn't.

Lena's mammá knows all about Octavio but says the memories escape her whenever she asks, and Lena understands her mammá's not the kind of woman who chases answers. Instead watches television and crawls inside cans of beer. Octavio's room is how he left it, dirty clothes in the hamper and dust covering everything. Lena remembers the picture of Octavio's girlfriend beside his bed, her wearing tight clothes and bending over, butt in the air and tits dangling like fruit ready to drop from a tree. Lena wrote a poem for her, slid it inside the frame: Two boys gone and a girl more still.

The comida comes, hamburger buns toasted with butter and patties sizzling, cheese dripping along the sides. Lena pours chile verde over the meat and límon on the papitas, both from plastic bottles at the end of the table. Tungi eats without taking a moment to appreciate his food; he's sloppy and gets mustard on his shirt, licks his greasy fingers and slurps his milkshake.

Tungi tells Lena to dig in, not to be shy because with looks like hers she don't need to worry about nothing, but Lena worries all the time. Now about being down— locked down like her brother or down-and-out like mammá? Will she fall as far as her father who booked when she was five but who can rot in hell for all anyone cares? Lena takes a bite; the chile makes her face sweat, tongue burn and eyes water.

Tungi's sorry to hear about Octavio, sorry for her loss, and Lena thinks about Octavio dying. She knows the date, wonders about his last meal and the final thought he'll be asked to spill, how the chance to choose the last words of your life is the scariest thing she can think of. Most condemned apologize to the families they've broken and praise Jesús. Lena knows no matter what Octavio manages to say, his words will belong to her. To repeat and change until she can make sense of them. She hears Octavio talking in her ear: I'm ready to go. Lena's ready, too.

Lena pushes her food aside, surprises Tungi. He mentions how he's heard she could put a lot away, and Lena tells him he has no idea. Tungi laughs and says he needs the toilet. He rocks himself from the booth and knocks over what's left of Lena's milkshake, the pink slush sliding across the table. Tungi wipes the crumbs from his shirt, promises a quick piss and a trip back to his place. He smiles and Lena takes the folded paper from her pocket, wipes the mess back inside the cup. The ink bleeds and words dissolve as the page soaks itself blank again. Lena leaves the restaurant with Tungi still in the bathroom. She walks toward the mountains that are somehow darker than the sky and thinks about paper turning soft and easy to tear.

San Efrén Maldonado

Efrén closed his eyes and felt his body float ever so slightly above his seat. With his eyes pressed shut Efrén decided he would one day fly to the moon, wanting to make his own giant leaps for mankind.

San José Cupertino

Memorial – September 18

Patronage

Air Crews

Air Travelers

Aircraft Pilots

Astronauts

Aviators

Flyers

Paratroopers

Students

Test Takers

Prayer: Dear ecstatic Conventual Saint who patiently bore calumnies, your secret was Christ the crucified Savior who said: When I will be lifted up I will draw all peoples to myself. You were always spiritually lifted up. Give aviators courage and protection, and may they always keep in mind your greatly uplifting example.

Efrén Maldonado wasn't smart enough. That's what his teachers told him, the kids in class and school guidance counselor, even Efrén's mammá. He'd failed Life Sciences and Pre-Algebra and bombed World History. English wasn't a total loss but one C wasn't enough to make a good semester. Efrén would flunk freshman year if he didn't pick things up. On the walk home from school, sun setting behind the mountains and leaving him in the dark, Efrén carried his history book and extra credit assignments, but after being told he'd never be an astronaut—would be lucky to finish high school—Efrén had a hard time caring about history or the world. For him the moon was all that mattered.

Efrén loved the moon, had been so in love with the white rock that he never listened to the stupid talk about full moons making people crazy or believing what his grammá told him; that the devil lived on the dark side, El Diablo tricking people into looking for him without knowing. The romance had started in elementary school, the morning after a space shuttle exploded into streaks of light and crashed from the sky. The blast had been replayed on television most of the day and night, Efrén unable to stop watching the national disaster before his mammá finally made him go to bed. She looked sad telling Efrén to sleep, but that was the way she always looked.

The next day Efrén and his classmates were led into the school auditorium, seated in rows of creaky wooden chairs. The room stuffy, air wet and stinking like mold, the place quiet with everyone waiting. A television had been wheeled to the auditorium floor where the school orchestra and band performed recitals. Where PE classes played dodge ball if it rained. A grainy video was played, a copy of a copy of the first moon landing. The rebroadcast was something the principal cooked up to make the students feel better. Mr. Ward, Efrén's third grade teacher with his thick plastic glasses and sweat stains constantly under his arms, explained this to them afterward, then went on to complain how the government shouldn't be spending money on trips to nowhere in the first place.

But the moon didn't seem like nowhere to Efrén. The black and white footage popped and hissed like scenes from an old sci-fi movie, and like sci-fi the moon seemed the perfect danger. The astronauts bounced as they skipped across the dusty surface, men learning to fly, darkness surrounding them. They were both supermen and sitting ducks. Efrén closed his eyes and felt his body float ever so slightly above his seat. With his eyes pressed shut Efrén decided he would one day fly to the moon, wanting to make his own giant leaps for mankind.

The apartment was empty when Efrén arrived home. In fact the whole neighborhood seemed missing, all the power out. Porch and streetlights off, nobody hanging on street corners or yellow lights glowing from bedroom windows. All the action was in the night sky, stars so bright Efrén could see out across the city from his bedroom window. By now Efrén new all about earths only satellite, the different phases, the thin atmosphere and magma oceans. Layers of water underneath the surface. Efrén climbed to the apartment roof and looked through his binoculars, a pair he'd gotten as a birthday gift instead of the telescope he wanted. The moon was as big as he'd ever seen, like a plugged in bulb brighter than even the stars.

From what Efrén could tell, the angel must have come from somewhere in Juárez. Launched from a dark spot he'd never been to. The angel started as a streak of fire cutting across the sky, embers peeling from the burning center and floating away until stopping midflight, the center a gleaming white disk. The angel spread his wings, the dark outline motionless across the lunar surface before falling back to earth.

Efrén shut his eyes, wanting to burn the vision in his memory, the wings long and powerful, the angel's body skinny and weak like his own. Again Efrén began to float, drifted from the roof and over the courtyard. The dry fountain and concrete slab. Branches of mesquite trees seeming to reach for him. Efrén never opened his eyes that day in the auditorium, too afraid to find out he wasn't flying, but this time Efrén had to know. He looked down and saw the ground speeding toward him, crashed halfway inside the fountain and the cement ground, snapping his leg, bone ripping through skin. Efrén cried from pain and joy, happy to know there was another way for him to get to the moon.

Santiago Matamoros

Memorial – July 25

Patronage

Druggists

Horsemen

Knights

Laborers

Pilgrims

Riders

Soldiers

Prayer: O Glorious Saint James, because of your fervor and generosity Jesus chose you to witness his glory on the Mount and his agony in the Garden. Obtain for us strength and consolation in the unending struggles of this life. Help us to follow Christ constantly and generously, to be victors over all our difficulties, and to receive the crown of glory in heaven.

"For give me Father for I'm about to sin. It's been long since my last confession. Since I was a kid."

"You're about to sin?"

Padre Maldonado didn't recognize the voice of the man in his confessional. He sounded young, not a teenager but not much older. Booze on his breath. Padre Maldonado tried to force himself fully awake, breathed deep through his nose and wondered how long he'd been out. If the man heard his snoring echoing in the empty church. Padre Maldonado had wanted to skip his duties in the confessional, his daily hour in the box at the hottest time of day. Once inside the heat had slipped his body into sleep like sugar dissolving into coffee.

"I'm going to kill a woman. I don't know her, if that makes a difference. I'm also going to abandon my wife and son, my baby-girl. My son will turn gangbanger and stab a boy behind a liquor store. My daughter's still young when the vision stops. I don't know what happens to her. I doubt anything good. These will be my sins, Father."

"A vision?" Padre Maldonado asked, now wanting to go back to sleep.

"Yes priest. I get them every night."

"These dreams you're having?"

"Yes priest."

"So you haven't killed anyone?"

"Not yet, priest, but soon."

Padre Maldonado didn't know any killers but was sure the man confessing wasn't one, liked to think he could spot evil if it knelt in front of him. Still, the man had a weight on him. The way he kept his fingers locked tightly together, head bent and wanting prayer. The man obviously guilty of something.

"I will do these things, priest. I've seen everything happen."

"Dreams are not sins."

"I thought bad thoughts were sins?"

"Well, they are, but you cannot control dreams. They are not real thoughts." Padre Maldonado didn't know if what he was saying was true. If there was a difference between thinking evil and dreaming it up. "The real sin would be to actually do these things. You have free will."

"No seas *pendejo*. Not even Jesus had free will. Who wants to get nailed to two-by-fours, *cabrón*?"

Padre Maldonado had felt the pull of fate, destiny or whatever the force was, tugging him for as along as he could remember, from high school to seminary and now here. He agreed with the man even though he knew it was against the company line. People had no free will. They were doomed to their parts in the story.

"I need penance, priest. You have to give it to me."

"Just don't do these things. Please don't do them."

The man became quiet for a moment, then squeezed his hands tight and started to pray: Señor mío, Jesucristo, Dios y Hombre verdadero, Creador, Padre y Redentor mío.

In the dream the man was a soldier, though he wasn't in the army and had no clue what would make him join—if he was forced or somehow his mind came around to the idea. After boot camp the man was shipped to war, not as a grunt but a mechanic. He carried a rifle along with a leather bag of loose tools and spare parts. Every night the man dreamt of fixing a stalled cargo truck in the middle of a crowded street. His patrol watching him swap a jumped timing chain. They were downtown, a bombed-out center with crushed buildings and men selling candy and cigarettes from the backs of trucks, live chickens and machetes.

While adjusting the chain the man caught sight of the woman he was doomed to kill. She looked like she might have been pregnant, maybe a new mother, body round but strong. Her face was beautiful, perfect smooth skin and teeth so white they looked blue around the edges. She charged the patrol from behind a fruit stand, a dead tree branch raised over her head and then smashed down on a soldier before anyone noticed her coming. The soldier looked dead as he collapsed to the ground—the vato didn't even move as she ran at him, like he wanted her to kill him.

The man described what happened after the soldier went down, how he couldn't remember thinking. Only felt his insides pulling away. His brain and gut and heart sucked through the bottoms of his feet until he was hollow. The confessor pointed his weapon at the woman and fired. She never saw him take aim or the round burst through her chest. The sky and sun probably the last thing the woman saw while knocked to her back and bleeding out.

Padre Maldonado wanted the man to stop, but he kept talking, about becoming a washed-up vet, a drunk married to a woman he hadn't met but knew he loved. The man said he didn't know his future wife's name or what she looked like, only the sound of her voice. The man cried when he talked about the children, a boy who was sweet but turned hard and a girl smart enough to be anything but probably settling for nothing.

When the man finished he and Padre Maldonado were silent, the priest thinking how clear the dream had been. Nothing fake about the remorse and regret in the man's voice. Padre Maldonado told the man the Lord worked in mysterious ways. Padre Maldonado said this all the time, was even how he used to explain the angel he'd seen as a boy. Only this time the line seemed more like a cheap way to explain what he couldn't. Padre Maldonado made the sign-of-the-cross and told the man to go in peace. The man thanked him and for the first time in a long time Padre Maldonado believed in repentance.

San Uriel Arcángel

Memorial – July 28

Patronage

None

Prayer: None

Nobody, not even Padre Maldonado, recognized the angel when he came to Mass. For years he sat in back, even when the pews were empty. He never stayed for the whole ritual. Didn't take Communion or pray. The angel came because he felt bad about the way things had turned out, little Efrén seeing him that night and getting the stupid idea to turn priest. The angel had been doing a favor for a friend and when finished crashed and burned onto the side of a mountain. Bones broken, spine snapped in three places. His wings singed and bloodied, the worst he'd been since the old days. That was a lesson the angel always had to relearn, that helping hurt in the worst way. Still, the angel knew he now had to watch over the priest, take care of the dumb kid who stared at the moon and saw what he thought was fate.

San Sebastián

Memorial – March 20

<u>Patronage</u>

Against Enemies of Religion

Bookbinders

Dying People

Hardware Stores

Plague

Prayer: Saint Sebastián, who did fortify those wavering in their faith, pray for us. Saint Sebastián, who did encourage the doubting to persevere to the end, pray for us. Saint Sebastián, who, in flamed with the love of God, did despise the pains inflicted by the tyrant, pray for us. Saint Sebastián, surrounded by celestial light, pray for us. Saint Sebastián, instructed by the holy angels, pray for us. Saint Sebastián, giving speech to the dumb, pray for us. Saint Sebastián, who for defending the truth was wounded by arrows, pray for us. Saint Sebastián, who was put to death with clubs, pray for us.

In the confessional Luis told Padre Maldonado, "Father, I've been told by an angel to leave my wife, to disappear, but before that I had to come see you."

Padre Maldonado paused for a moment, his mind turning back to that night he witnessed the angel rising toward the moon. "Luis, go back home to Perla."

"I can't do that. It's not her destiny. Not yours either."

"What are you talking about, Luis? Why are you here?"

Luis usually found himself at confession after one of his affairs, feeling guilt as bad as his want for sex, but this time he hadn't broken his vows. He explained how the angel had come to him at work, while he was making a pair of snakeskin boots. The angel looked like an old man, a bum really, dirty oily face and yellow fingernails, stunk like booze and armpit. The angel threatened to drop Luis from the sky if he didn't do what he'd been told.

"You're talking crazy," Padre Maldonado said. "An angel didn't come see you. Probably just some meth head." Padre Maldonado hadn't thought of the angel in years, except on the occasion when he was filled with regret for believing in god in the first place. "You didn't see any angels. No one sees them."

"I can see the end of the world when I close my eyes. Everything is cold and freezing rain never stops, valleys get flooded and water rises until covering mountains. Everywhere is white frozen lakes and suicidal birds nose-diving into them, exploding. I can't sleep."

"Go home, Luis. See a shrink. A curandero if that doesn't help."

"The angel said your gonna be a saint, moon-boy."

"What?"

Luis jumped through the confessional, pinned Padre Maldonado against the wall. The priest instinctively pinched his eyes shut and suddenly became light in Luis' grip, like he would float away if he let go, but Luis didn't, instead beat Padre Maldonado in the head and face. Busting cartilage and bone. Blood poured from Padre Maldonado's mouth and nose and eye sockets. The priest choked on a piece of bitten off tongue. There was screaming as Luis tossed the priest from the confessional, choruses of earsplitting shrieks as the body glided like a feather to the ground.

Santa Cecilía

Memorial – November 22

Patronage

Composers

Martyrs

Musicians

Poets

Singers

Prayer: Dear Saint Cecilía, one thing we know for certain about you is that you became a heroic martyr in fidelity to your divine bridegroom. We do not know that you were a musician but we are told that you heard angels sing. Inspire musicians to gladden the hearts of people by filling the air with God's gift of music and reminding them of the divine Musician who created all beauty.

While in a coma Efrén remembered falling for

Lola. She was the kind of girl a boy never got over, not only because of her looks—she was fine as hell, an ass made for crying over and legs that could walk forever—but because everything about her haunted like a ghost. She floated back and forth in Efrén's memory. His first real crush and kiss. First and only fuck. She'd lived in the same apartment building as Efrén but went to a different school. To Father Yermo, a private school her padres spent all their money on. Lola had no problem being near Efrén when her friends weren't around but did when they were. She'd laughed the day Efrén asked her to be his lady, Lola and her circle of snobby girlfriends smoking by the still busted water fountain. The next morning she smiled and waved at Efrén while waiting for the bus.

Years later, at her wedding, Lola seemed happy and comfortable. Not like Efrén remembered her. Lola introduced him to her friends and family. Her mother and father remembered Efrén from the building but not as a friend of Lola's. Efrén and Lola danced one song at the reception, Lionel Richie's Dancing on the Ceiling. Lola told Efrén that him being a priest was the strangest thing to her. When the song was over Efrén watched Lola's husband, a young but serious looking doctor, come and twirl her away.

San Uriel Arcángel

Memorial – July 28

Twitching Heart

The angel visited the priest at the hospital. He had lost an eye and a piece of tongue, but he would recover. The swelling eventually going down and bruises fading. Uriel couldn't heal the priest, making things better wasn't something he'd ever done. At first there'd been lots of visitors at the priest's bedside, flowers and balloons and veladoras, but after months of him being unconscious they quit coming. Lives moved on. Most of them, anyway. The angel had nowhere to go and waited at the side of the priest, knowing the end was in sight.

San Valentín de Roma

Memorial – February 14

Matt Méndez

Happy Marriages

Love

Travelers

Young People

Prayer: Dear Lord, who art high in the heavens, giver of love and passion, who strings the heart's cords. It is only true hearts that can create a masterpiece. So let the lovers remember that their soul's desire is a lighted fire, created to be the Art of the Lovers; the art of two into one.

Linda and Oscar were in town for Christmas, newly dating and shopping for gifts at a used bookstore. Oscar sat in a dirty armchair and read the newspaper. An article on the anniversary of the still comatose priest. Oscar remembered the miracle girl from when he was a boy, how after the day at her house his parents split for good. For him that was the end of family and faith, and he liked to pretend he'd never had either. His pretending had served him well, his lonesomeness having attracted Linda to him in the first place. Both of them birds without flocks. Linda ran her fingers along a row of fiction, felt a naked hardcover and stopped. Linda pulled the book from the shelf. The book was Pedro Páramo, a novel Linda had read many times but was too sad to be her favorite. The name, Perla, was carved across the back.

Oscar surprised Linda by telling her he'd seen the

hardback before. It was his mother's.

"How'd it get here?" Linda asked.

"I sold it at a yard sale, years ago. Must have been soled again. I guess no one likes it." Linda handed Oscar the book. He thumbed to the last page and showed Linda his old address written in the corner. "I can't believe this book is here."

"Did you ever read it?"

"Nope."

"It's kind of like a miracle, us finding it here."

Linda told Oscar how she loved bookstores, especially used ones, the musty smell and volumes of dog-eared paperbacks with coffee stained pages. Now she loved missing cover jackets and personal notes written in the margins. Oscar put the thin tome back on the shelf, said he hated the informal economy of the bookstore but liked the quiet. He didn't mention that miracles, like fate, were bullshit.

Linda was a Lorna Dee Cervantes geek and had already decided to name her first-born daughter after the poet, but she liked the name Perla, too. Maybe for a second girl or if not then a grandchild. Linda liked the idea of creating history in this way, pictured herself a happy old woman as Lorna handed down the book, the name, and maybe a poem:

When summer ended

the leaves of snapdragons withered

taking their shrill-colored mouths with them.

They were still, so quiet. They were

violet where umber now is. She hated

and she hated to see

them go. Flowers

born when the weather was good - this

she thinks of, watching the branch of peaches

daring their ways above the fence, and further,

two hummingbirds, hovering, stuck to each other,

arcing their bodies in grim determination

to find what is good, what is

given them to find. These are warriors

distancing themselves from history.

They find peace

in the way they contain the wind

and are gone.

Together Linda and Oscar shopped, buying puzzle and cookbooks. A mushy vampire novel, just to see what all the hype was about. Before leaving the bookstore Linda walked back to the fiction section and grabbed Pedro Páramo from the shelf, slipped it into her purse and zipped it shut. She did this slowly, making sure Oscar was watching. Linda's first love, a boy named Juan, had once stolen a car for her birthday. It was bright red with a sunroof, the nicest he could find. Juan took Linda joyriding but was caught the next day. Linda never saw Juan again—her parents putting a restraining order on him and shipping her to live with her tía and primo in New Mexico. The stolen car was the best present Linda had ever received. To find out love was a crime, to keep it going was risk after risk.

Oscar looked nervous as they left the bookstore but placed his hand into Linda's. The two drove away without saying a word, but Linda knew they were now partners in crime.

San Lucas

Memorial – October 18

Patronage

Artists

Bachelors

Doctors

Physicians

Unmarried Men

Prayer: Most charming and saintly physician, you were animated by the heavenly Spirit of love. In faithfully detailing the humanity of Jesus, you also showed his divinity and his genuine compassion for all human beings. Inspire our physicians with your professionalism and with the divine compassion for their patients. Enable them to cure the ills of both body and spirit that afflict so many in our day.

Dr. Jorge had been the one to notice the babies getting smaller, remembered the first one to grab his attention. The baby boy looked normal, furry backed and clumsy, like most of the healthy babies Dr. Jorge had delivered. Yet there was something missing from him. Dr. Jorge weighed the baby at 3,325 grams, exactly the average. He sent the baby home with proud parents but made note of the weight in his personal records. Dr. Jorge did the same for all births after that, tracked each one while making sure to factor for poverty, bad prenatal habits, lack of healthcare and education. He would have to wait for the numbers to stack up, but he was sure each baby he delivered was lighter than the one before.

Eventually Dr. Jorge had enough numbers to crunch, and the results were what he'd feared. With each baby delivered, from baby girl to boy, were fractions of grams lost. From 3,325 grams to 3,324.5 to 3,324.05 and dropping. He studied the spreadsheet he'd created, tracked weights by months and years. The numbers tiny but real. Babies were lessening, but that wasn't the only thing Dr. Jorge noticed. There was another problem. The number of shrinking babies born each month was also shrinking. The average number of infants born per year slipping, just slightly, by fractions.

It was time to worry, and Dr. Jorge worried. He wanted to sound the alarms, but Dr. Jorge's friends and colleagues warned him to keep quiet and not go deep into the numbers. Birthrates moved in cycles. The shifts were negligible and besides there were too many fucking people on the goddamn planet anyway. They told him that just because uterine cancer took his wife it didn't mean he was an expert in all signs of loss. Knowing he had to do something, Dr. Jorge wrote a paper called "Say Goodbye, Baby." It went unpublished. Dr. Jorge had written it longhand, in verse, a twenty page Sestina that tried to make the numbers into something more, but words weren't enough, either.

Years later, when the birthrate plunged and infant mortality shot up—babies born missing more than grams, missing arms and legs, genitals—Dr. Jorge had been long retired. The doctor knew he was only a small time physician and the problem facing the world much bigger than him. He was not a prophet. Not a poet. His warning to watch out for shrinking babies never heard.

San Juan María Vianney

Memorial – August 4

Patronage

Confessors

Parish Priests

Prayer: Saintly Pastor of Ars and splendid model of all servants of souls, you were considered not very bright, but you possessed the wisdom of the Saints. You were a true pontifex, a bridge-builder, between God and his people as countless penitents streamed to your confessional. Inspire all priests to be dedicated mediators between God and his people in our day.

Blind in one eye, the tip of his tongue missing, Padre Maldonado decided the confessional was where he belonged. After twenty years in a coma, the parish long ago brining another priest and wanting Padre Maldonado to retire, Padre Maldonado returned and decided to stay. He opened the confessional fulltime, working sixteen hours a day, everyday, wanting to hear whatever anyone had to say.

He told the confessors who came to him to go in peace and had quit bothering with sins and guilt altogether. He listened to stories and told his own. Some about the moon. How maybe the devil had been there. Who the fuck knew? Tired of long lines at the confessional, of the spectacle and rumors of a floating heretic priest, the bishop wanted Padre Maldonado excommunicated, but luckily for the bishop the rains started. Storms came hard and stayed for days at a time. Then weeks and months. The mountain behind the church began to soften, the mud and rock one day avalanching the house of worship and burying Padre Maldonado inside. Free of the priest, the bishop declared the parish a danger and ordered it closed forever.

San Uriel Arcángel

Memorial – July 28

Patronage

None

Prayer: None

Efrén was finally able to recognize the angel as the seraph dug through the frozen ground and rock and pulled him from the collapsed confessional—where the priest had been waiting, as usual, when the earth came sliding. The ground was now covered with snow, the church walls crumbled away, the priest almost a hundred years old. Unable to move, the angel held Efrén in his arms. He noticed the angel's fingernails were packed with black muck, his arms lined with thick scars. Wings bald and pink. Efrén didn't have to close his eyes this time to feel gravity slip and his body beginning to soar. The angel took flight and carried the priest through the gray clouds that blanketed the sky. Efrén could see the sun behind them. Bright but not blinding. They effortlessly moved through the atmosphere until the angel's wings caught fire. They singed and popped, crackled into black embers. The angel's body continued to burn and remained ablaze until it was completely consumed and thinned into smoke that continued upward. The smoke smelled like incense. Without the angel supporting him the priest also continued to rise, the glowing sun getting closer and becoming clear. The warmth of the smoldering globe seemed to welcome Efrén Maldonado, and the old priest was surprised to discover it was indeed the sun, and not the moon, that he'd been wanting all along.

The Last Ones on Earth

How could Elco not give a fuck? A baby was a miracle, and not the pretend kind baby making used to be.

Elco Lozano drove west on I-10, went slow to avoid the ruts and potholes left by the rains. Elco didn't want to make the trip. It was dangerous. Perla, his daughter, sat next to him, not saying much underneath a blanket and glued to a book. Perla didn't talk much after her mother, Elco's ex-wife Lorna, and stepfather swerved off Scenic Drive and crashed down the Franklin Mountains. Perla moved in with Elco after the funeral but he hardly saw her, Perla either locked in her room or disappearing for days at a time. She had no use for Elco, and he was surprised she'd even bothered to tell him the news at all. He'd been doing piecework in the backyard, rebuilding a set of heavy double doors, reinforcing them with wrought iron, when Perla marched outside and declared: Not that you give a fuck, but I'm probably pregnant.

How could Elco not give a fuck? A baby was a miracle, and not the pretend kind baby making used to be. Life had gone missing on the planet, vegetation only growing in small patches of land—bananas in Somalia and Ecuador, wheat and corn in Japan and Peru. Of course nothing grew in the Southwest, just one saguaro cactus somewhere in Arizona, where Elco and Perla were now driving. Elco had heard no woman had gotten pregnant in over a year, the last one born with no arms or legs, no privates.

The road was pitted with gaping holes and rolled into the mountain, disappearing into the haze that hung like a wet blanket. Elco didn't know how long the trip would be but packed heavy: bottles of distilled water and freeze-dried noodles, vitamin and mineral supplements, fresh bananas with protein extract. He was ready if the car broke down, with a filled gas can and full spare, a .9mm tucked into the waistband of his pants. The cops didn't cruise the highway anymore, instead worked the edges of the city—the government, still worried about borders.

"Pull over," Perla said. She tossed the book to the floor and wrestled out of her blanket. "I'm gonna barf."

"Can you hold it?" There were stories of people killed on the side of the road, bodies stripped and dumped. Dirty clothes apparently as valuable as money. Elco drove faster.

"Fine," Perla said, rolling down the window and leaning out, feet dangling over the seat.

"Shit Perla!"

Perla sprayed vomit along the side of the car. Perla's beginning to round belly peeked from underneath her sweater as she twisted back inside. She was twelve weeks, ready to be done with puking, and Elco worried about the baby going bad inside her.

"I don't think this is good. Maybe there's something

wrong with the baby."

"Jesus, why would you say that?" Perla wiped her mouth, drool sticking to her sleeve. "I'm gonna go again. Pull over!"

He pulled onto the shoulder and cut the lights, couldn't see more than a few feet into the fog. Perla ran from the car, disappearing, and Elco went after her, panicked until he found her vomiting on a patch of frozen tumbleweeds, the icy thorns melting under the heat. Elco was sure they were somewhere in Las Cruces, though the road signs had long been stolen or painted over with what seemed to be warnings. Stick-figure men with Xs over them, crude skulls with gaping black eyeholes. It started to sprinkle.

After Perla told Elco she might be pregnant he took her to see Dr. Jorge, the same doctor who checked Lorna when she'd been pregnant with Perla. Lorna had kept in touch with Dr. Jorge, like she did with everyone, sent him birthday and Christmas cookies. At Lorna's funeral Dr. Jorge hugged Elco, squeezed him good in the ribs and said: I know you loved her. Probably the only reason you're alive. If you ever need anything, carnal, just ask. Dr. Jorge was retired but still had connections at a clinic downtown, and he snuck Elco and Perla through the backdoor of La Promesa without asking too many questions. He had Perla pee in a cup, took her weight and blood pressure, examined her eyes, ears, and everything else. Dr. Jorge explained that if Perla were pregnant—a big if carnalito, things are going down the tubes in a hurry—they'd have to keep her pregnancy a secret, protect her and the baby from all the whackos bound to pop up.

A car zoomed past in the opposite direction, probably to El Paso but Elco couldn't think why. "Feeling better?" Elco asked, crouched beside Perla. Dr. Jorge had called the house with the positive results, must have forgotten his science when he asked Perla just how she'd managed to get pregnant. Perla had been on the computer, didn't even look away from the glowing screen when she answered: By fucking. How did you think babies are made? That answered the question for Elco, too.

"We should go back," Elco said. "I'll take you to see the doc."

"No, I'm going to see the saguaro," Perla said, walking away from Elco like she planned to hump it all the way to Arizona. "I have to make this trip. You wouldn't understand."

They were on their way to see the saguaro Perla found on YouTube, a video of the cactus in front of a plywood wall. Christmas lights wrapped around the body and upturned arms, flickering red and green. There was a man in the video; a guy Elco recognized even while bundled in a camouflage parka, the old service issue with an uneven cross stitched to the front. His name was Chapo Tapia, Elco's old boss from the army, from the forgotten African Wars; Chapo spoke directly into the camera. We're the last ones on earth. Blessed are those who take heart.

The sprinkling turned to rain as a pair of headlights flicked on in the distance, the beams of light growing wide as a truck rushed toward Perla. Elco lost Perla in the glow and grabbed his pistol, ran blindly to find her. Elco hadn't fired anything more dangerous than a bottle rocket since the war, since killing a boy while on patrol. The truck skidded to a stop in front of Perla, and three silhouetted figures quickly piled out. Elco shouted for Perla to run to the car and get inside, but Perla froze, the rain turning harder.

Moving closer Elco realized the attackers weren't a gang but a family, a sickly looking father and mother, two teenage boys with starved faces. The mother stayed in the cabin of the truck, her hands gripping the wheel, wipers whooshing. The father yelled at the boys to ignore the girl and get what was inside the trunk. The father looked like the old men Elco's shop used to hire for sanding and finishing chairs, the old-timers too weak for the manual stuff but needing work. The younger boy, holding a baseball bat, stood next to Perla—he would be the first one shot; his older brother, wielding a machete, ran to the car and popped the trunk. He would get it next and finally the father, who walked toward Elco with a crowbar in his hand. Picking them off would be easy—Elco had been a marksman with the M-16 and .9mm—but Elco didn't want to shoot anyone. Keeping his gun on the father he tried to look as desperate as the bandit family, just wanting them to disappear as quickly as they'd arrived.

"You can have what's in the trunk," Elco said. "But then you leave us alone."

"What are you saying?" Perla said, coming back to her senses. "That's all our supplies."

"Perla, get in the car," Elco said. "And put on your goddamn coat!"

The mother honked her horn, probably not liking the look of Elco's pistol, and motioned for the father to retreat, but the father didn't move, the crowbar tight in his hand. Perla slowly got inside the car as the bandit family remained still.

Elco unloaded the supplies inside the trunk as the two boys retreated to their mother. The father stood alone in the rain and watched as Elco jumped inside his car.

"So now what?" Perla asked.

"We keep going," Elco said. "That's what you want, right?" Elco wanted to head home now more than ever but knew Perla would later risk the trip alone. She was just like Lorna, and if Lorna were alive she'd be the one driving to Arizona. Not everything is always so ugly, Lorna used to say. Elco looked back at the father now being whipped by the storm and wondered if she might have been wrong.

They drove, and Elco got to thinking. How both the world and his life had gone so wrong. No one was exactly sure what had happened to the planet. Most scientists blamed the crazy switch in weather patterns for freezing North America, argued how it could've been prevented. Others said the change had to do with electromagnetic waves and bioengineering, too many dudes in white lab coats screwing with gametes and chlorophyll photoreceptors—whatever that meant. For Elco the end came when Lorna left him, said she could no longer be married to a casualty. The African Wars were long over but still crippled Elco, not with disfigured bones or scarred skin, missing limbs or organs. He looked normal enough on the outside, no sign of the creeping desperation that was now part of his DNA.

Anxiety was part of Perla's genetic make-up, too. That's why she emailed Chapo in the first place. Chapo's website was full of bible-talk. "I am the Alpha and the Omega," says the Lord God, "who is, and who was, and who is to come, the Almighty." Perla had mentioned Elco to Chapo in her message and soon an invitation for them to visit had been extended. Perla probably thought there would be an answer for her when she set her eyes on the cactus, from witnessing another life form still functioning in the old way, but Elco knew better. Perla and the saguaro were leftovers from an already gone era, not a second coming.

On the road Perla stared out the window as the rain turned to snow. Elco and Perla had only a couple of water bottles left, some snacks hidden in the glove box. Another run-in, like the one with the bandit family, and who knew what would happen. Elco hoped he was doing the right thing, but knowing what the right things were was never Elco's specialty.

Elco had been a senior in high school when his draft notice landed in the mail, but he didn't trash it like his friends had, didn't grab Lorna and go across the line, bags packed. Elco reported to the mass briefing and enlisted. Are you sure? Lorna had asked after. We can still make a run for it. Elco told Lorna that he had to go, that he couldn't live his life running away, but the truth was Elco was too afraid to do anything else. The night before he left for boot camp Lorna dozed-off with her head on his chest, drool soaked on Elco's shirt and the weight of her body pressed his arm into pins-and-needles. His last comfortable sleep.

Deploying after boot camp, Elco had been in Nampula twelve months, on another steamy afternoon patrol when he killed the boy. Elco's uniform had been soaked after humping miles of coastline, a soggy letter from Lorna in his pocket. Chapo had been leading the patrol when he spotted a group of insurgents through his binoculars. They were over a ridge, by the water supply. The insurgents looked like dots from where Elco stood, like they could be anyone. That's the way the whole war seemed to Elco, no one ever knowing who or where the enemy was, what they were doing or when the fighting would be over.

Going against the rules of engagement, Chapo didn't get on the radio and call for surveillance, didn't ask permission. Chapo came to Elco, his "brother from another mother," and squeezed his shoulder and walked him away from the unit. Let's see how good a shot you really are. Elco and Chapo were the only browns in the unit, and Elco felt a loyalty to him, had Chapo's back when whites and blacks talked shit about him, even though he too thought Chapo was a barbero. Take one down, Chapo ordered, pointing to the water bladders beyond the ridge. We can't risk any tampering with the water supply. Elco had been in firefights before, knew it was sometimes better to shoot first and ask questions later. Better to be wrong than dead. Elco lifted his weapon, stopped on the first still shadow that fell in his line-of-sight and squeezed the trigger.

"I'm hungry," Perla said. Elco hadn't seen another car since leaving Las Cruces, only the remains of abandoned towns, rotted wood shacks and empty buildings, vacant parking lots and crashed cars in ditches. "And I have to pee."

"Don't piss out the window," Elco said. "We gotta find a good place this time. No more dumb risks. Play it safe from here on out."

Elco had already been playing safe with Perla, taking her to Dr. Jorge's house once a week, and Dr. Jorge would take Perla into his kitchen, where he kept machines and equipment he'd stolen from a shutdown hospital, and give a check-up. Perla didn't want Elco with her, leaving him alone in the living room where he read files Dr. Jorge left on his desk. Elco learned about chemicals in dust: alkylphenol, which acted like estrogen but ruined sexual development, phthalate, a chemical that screwed with the reproductive systems in animals. Elco imagined Perla breathing invisible poisons and them going straight for the baby, leaving a miniature skeleton floating in his daughter's belly.

"You see anything out there?" Elco asked. Perla wiped steam from the passenger window, her reflection seeming to float outside the car. Perla had been a little girl when Lorna and Elco split—Lorna had tried to keep the family together, first counseling and then church, but Elco's ability to keep anything together had sunk like a rock to the bottom of a cloudy river. In those days he went weeks without speaking; he rarely ate, couldn't sleep or concentrate, keep a schedule or a promise. Lorna had always wanted Elco to open up, to tell her about the war, but Elco kept the memory of the boy and

151

the young woman to himself.

The young woman had surprised Elco while on patrol, ran at him from behind a fruit stand and bashed him on the head with a gnarled tree branch, downed it across Elco's Kevlar helmet, his rifle held useless against his chest as he dropped to the ground. Elco didn't see who shot the woman—never asked—but heard the pop of a rifle, the thud of a body hitting the ground next to him. The gurgle in her throat as she took her last breaths.

"There's a light flashing," Perla said.

A neon light flickered through the fog, just off the highway. Elco hoped the sign was from a safe place, one with food—if anyone was there at all.

"Let's check it out," Elco said.

The light was from a sign that flashed Concha's Diner. The building was brick, painted yellow with a mural of La Virgen half done on the wooden front door. The Virgen's face was missing, an empty outline underneath a blue shawl, half painted roses. There was a car parked in front, covered in mud and frost, the windows tinted, one shattered and held together by the black film. Four flat tires. Elco took off his coat and handed it to Perla.

"Put this one on too, the blanket over that," Elco said. He got out of the car. "I'll come get you if it's tranquilo."

"I don't want to wait here," Perla said, tightening the blanket around her shoulders. "I want to go inside."

"Who knows what's in there," Elco said.

"I'm not staying in here."

Perla struggled from the car and made her way toward the diner, but this time Elco stopped her before she could go inside. "Just stay behind me," Elco said, adjusting the pistol behind his back. "I used to be a soldier. I can protect you."

"I know. That's all I know about you," Perla said. "My daddy the broken soldier."

The wooden door was heavy but unlocked, and a bell rang as they walked inside. Tables and chairs lined the walls of the diner, booths in the corners. Table settings at each one. A radio buzzed static, a man's voice underneath the hiss. The diner didn't seem like a real restaurant, more like a depiction of one put together by somebody who'd only read about restaurants in books.

"Welcome to Concha's?"

A woman popped out from behind the counter. She looked to be the same age as Perla but wasted, like the boys from the bandit family, skinny in the body and face, but what Elco couldn't stop looking at was her tattoo, a greening black widow with spindly legs covering one side of her shaved head, a web on the other. She was a spider woman, Elco thought.

"Are you Concha?" Elco asked.

"Nope," the spider woman said. "That bitch is long gone."

"My daughter needs the bathroom," Elco said. He could feel Perla holding her breath behind him. Her holding on to his arm, squeezing.

"No way, bro," the spider woman said, her voice sounding familiar, like Elco was someone she knew but didn't like. The spider woman stepped forward and pulled a knife, a stubby utility blade that curved like a beak near the point, the teeth sharp and crossed. Elco stepped back, bumped Perla who gripped him harder. The spider woman's arms were scarred, old looking tattoos cut into, dug out. Scar tissue scrambled over twists of ink. "You order something or get the fuck out."

Elco eased Perla into a booth and sat beside her. A buffer between her and the spider woman. Elco tried to listen to the radio, but the words were too far, couldn't tell if the man was speaking English or Spanish. If it mattered. The spider woman put her knife away and disappeared into the kitchen. Elco knew he should've seized the moment and escaped, but it felt good having Perla close to him, even at knifepoint.

"I still have to piss," Perla said. "I mean pee."

Elco walked Perla to the bathroom and stood guard. He felt useful for the first time in a long time. Was glad to be the one taking Perla on this trip.

"Check this shit out." The spider woman returned from the kitchen carrying two plates. "You're the first two to try my special eggs."

"Put those on the table and back away," Elco said. He pulled his .9mm on the spider woman. The spider woman dropped the plates on the table, backed away while keeping watch on Elco as Perla emerged from the bathroom.

"What exactly were you trying to serve us?" Elco asked, knowing he and Perla needed to eat, now wishing he'd kept their supplies. The odor of cooked eggs reminded him of the chow hall at basic training, of the mess tent at the war, of hunger mixed with nerves. Slowly walking Perla back to the booth he noticed the eggs didn't look like anything he remembered, not fluffy or yellow and instead stringy and brown, floating in a pool of grease.

"Scrambled eggs," the spider woman answered. "You fucking deaf?"

"Where did you get eggs?" Perla asked. "I thought only the Dutch had chickens."

"Fuck the Dutch," the spider woman said.

"She didn't mean nothing," Elco said, trying to keep the spider woman calm; she was a different creature than the bandit family.

"I got the only supply of eggs left in the world." The spider woman stared at Perla. "What do you think of that, Miss Didn't Mean Nothing?"

"Show me where you got the eggs?" Elco motioned with the pistol and the spider woman walked back inside the kitchen, her hands in the air as if under arrest.

The spider woman led Elco and Perla outside the diner, to a bolted door around back. The wind blew, made it hard to stand. Elco hadn't actually planned on following the spider woman all the way outside. He'd wanted to get her alone, bust her on the head and ransack the place for supplies without Perla knowing, but Perla had again grabbed onto his arm and held tight as the spider woman led them through the kitchen. The spider woman had been abandoned by her own mother, been left alone too long and turned wild. Elco knew the same thing had been happening to him. Until Perla.

"There," the spider woman said, opening the door.

Elco peeked down the rotted staircase—making sure not to take his eyes off the spider woman for too long. He didn't see chickens or eggs inside the basement. Instead a mound of iguanas, a moving pile of green-ridged skin and prehistoric black eyes, of hooked claws digging into flesh as they crawled over each other like a mass grave come to life. The spider woman told Elco and Perla how her mother had found two iguanas nesting behind the staircase, took them as a bad sign and left for Chapo and the saguaro. Wanting God because everything else had disappeared. It wasn't long before the entire town followed and never came back.

"I fed them," the spider woman said. "Look at how many I have created. I'm going to be rich. Famous. I'm gonna show everyone." The spider woman grinned at Elco and Perla. "You're just like everyone else. Going to see that saguaro. To pray to some stupid plant? The fake preacher makes you pay to see it. Did you know that?"

"I'm not going to pray," Perla said. "I'm not interested in the science of it, either. I just want to see it. That's all."

"You're a fucking liar," the spider woman said. "You're like everyone else. Wanting miracles, wanting things to be like they were but that shit is over with. There is no more god to help you."

"You're right," Perla said. "I do want a miracle."

"What about my lizards. They're miracles. They make babies!"

"You eat their babies," Perla said.

"If your pops didn't have that pistol on me, I'd fucking eat you." The spider woman pulled her knife; her mouth clamped shut, the tattoo on her head creased into wrinkles.

"I'm pregnant," Perla yelled. "I want to one day tell my baby what I saw. That's the miracle I want."

"¡Mentirosa!" The spider woman screamed. "Those days are over!"

"Put the knife down," Elco said, keeping the pistol on the spider woman but she no longer cared. Dying wasn't the worst thing that could happen to her, so Elco aimed into the basement and fired. Blood bubbled from the pile of green bodies; the iguanas raced over and under each other, slammed into walls and wooden beams. The clicking and banging a sickening drum. Elco had hoped the spider woman would go to her babies, but instead she charged Elco, dug her dull blade deep into the meat of his shoulder. Elco dropped the pistol, and Perla screamed. Elco wrestled the spider woman down, slamming her hard on the dirt ground, her face thudding flat against it. She looked dead, her face and arms curled underneath her chest. Perla sobbed behind him.

Stepping back from the spider woman, Elco wobbled and fell. He looked on the ground for his gun but couldn't find it. Maybe he'd kicked it by accident during the struggle, sent the pistol skidding away; maybe it was under the spider woman. Perla knelt beside the spider woman and touched her stubbly head, Perla's fingers gentle as she traced over the tattoo. "We gotta get out of here," Elco said, not sure if the missing firearm was good or bad.

Perla sprinted back through the kitchen as Elco stopped to look through drawers and shelves, eventually finding a roll of cling wrap. Elco pulled off his sweater, the layers of shirts underneath, and wrapped the clear film over a folded shirt he'd pressed hard against the hole in his shoulder. He couldn't tell how bad the wound was but thought his field dress would stop the bleeding as long as he kept pressure on it, didn't move too much. Perla raced back into the kitchen and helped Elco pull back on his sweater, his arm burning as she touched him.

"Is it bad?" Perla asked. "We should go home."

"I'm fine," Elco said. "She barely nipped me."

"Come back!" The spider woman screamed from behind them. "Don't leave me here."

Elco pulled Perla through the diner and out the front door, relived the spider woman was alive but done taking any more chances with her. The spider woman stood at the front door as Elco and Perla drove away. Her nose crooked and split down the middle, beginning to swell with splattered blood across her chest. They skidded through the parking lot, past a fallen mesquite with its useless and exposed roots, its branches snapped by the ground.

"I didn't mean it," the spider woman said. "I believe you! I believe you!"

§§§

Arizona was covered in snow.

Chapo's compound was a tract home, a lone stucco box in the middle of a housing development that never got going. A ten-foot chain fence surrounded Chapo's lot, razor wire along the top. Cars lined the sides of the road leading to Chapo's, along with trash and burning campfires. Elco and Perla walked, finished the last of the water. Perla held her book, the thin novel squeezed between her fingers. Elco and Perla had ditched the car near the bottom of the mountain, the climb too steep and snow too thick. Elco hoped they'd be able to find it on their way back, that it wouldn't be lost to the winter that kept coming.

A small crowd—maybe thirty, maybe less—huddled around Chapo's fence, most facing the house but some against the wall that divided the backyard. A barrier made mostly of plywood but with sections of sheet metal and scrap—even cardboard—blocked the view to what Elco guessed was the saguaro. Elco and Perla walked toward the front of the house and stopped along the chained gate. The exterior of the house was badly damaged; chunks of missing stucco exposing the chicken wire and lathing underneath. The wooden pillars of the porch buckled and looked ready to collapse on the speakers and long folding table set-up by the front door. The table was covered with a serape, a leather-bound book resting on it. Elco could hear a man crying over a pack of dogs barking somewhere near the mountain. Another man had collapsed beside the gate; his family—Elco guessed—hovered over him, looked unsure of what to do.

The porch speakers loudly popped and then hummed, quieting everyone. Snow continued to fall. The front door slowly opened as Chapo emerged. He wore a red robe draped over his camouflage getup, the same cross stitched to the front; wrinkled pictures and prayer cards dangled across the seams along with milagros and strands of ribbon. Chapo's hair had gone thin and white, his neck saddled with droopy skin. Chapo looked viejo but somehow still a soldier, the cross like rank on his chest. Elco remembered the old army slogan from when he was a kid. An army of one. That's what Chapo was, not a soldier but a force onto himself.

"Let us pray."

There was a rush to the fence, the crowd pressing against Elco and Perla. Elco could smell their bodies, the rotting breath and oily skin. "Blessed is the one who reads the words of this prophecy, and blessed are those who hear it and take to heart what is written because the time is near. " Chapo picked up the book from the table and fanned the pages as he raised it over his head. "We are saved by these words, the last fruit and flowers blessed to my house. We are the last ones on earth."

Chapo led everyone in prayers, some Elco recognized, others he was sure his old sergeant had made up. The wind blew harder. Elco knew he should be close to freezing, but his shoulder burned, his body slicked with wetness. Elco looked at the praying faces, knew they were hoping for miracles or trying to get on the right side of god. Perla adjusted to get a better look and Elco almost fell, realized he'd been leaning on her. She wasn't praying, and Elco was glad she'd told the spider woman the truth. He looked for the man who'd collapsed against the fence and saw he'd been abandoned, his body quickly covered by a sheet of fresh white snow.

A young looking soldier, dressed like Chapo, swung open the gate. The small group briefly heaved backward, knocking Elco to the ground, before surging inside the compound. Elco tried to stand but couldn't find his feet, the earth slick and crunching underneath him. From the ground Elco watched as the gate pinned the fallen man against the fence, the sheet of snow cracking like a shell and showing the meat inside. Chapo's soldier did crowd control, pushed people into a line with the butt of his old hunting rifle. He looked like Chapo, and Elco wondered if he was his son. Perla knelt beside Elco, took off her blanket and coat and wrapped them around her father.

"You're shaking," Perla said. "We need to find a hospital."

"No," Elco said, feeling sweat continue to soak through his clothes. "I'm fine. Vamos."

Perla held Elco by his good arm, and he felt the

handle of his .9mm pressed against her hip as she helped him to Chapo's backyard. Perla sat Elco on a bench by the backdoor. She promised Elco she'd find help. As she ran off, Elco felt dripping from his arm. What he thought had been sweat turned out to be blood. He wiped his hand and shut his eyes.

Chapo and Elco had driven alone to the top of the ridge, the rest of the unit ordered to stand-fast. The insurgents had turned out to be a man and woman, a group of children, looking for water. Chapo parked the Humvee near the rubber bladders that looked like bloated stomachs ready to rupture. Water trucks filled the bladders once a week only the water wasn't for drinking—the poor family having no idea. The water was brackish, used by the field hospital to wash bloody sheets and scrub floors. To do laundry. Elco smelled the gunpowder cooking in the chamber of his weapon. There were no clouds in the sky, the sun like an open faucet that couldn't be shut off.

Leaving the engine running, Chapo sprang from the Humvee and ran to where Elco had fired. Elco already knew the boy was dead, remembered watching his head snap back with a burst and then collapse to the ground. Elco fixed himself with the barrel of his rifle butted against his cheek, but he couldn't steady his hands as he groped for the trigger and ended up tossing his weapon to the ground in frustration. He felt like he was on fire, his clothes searing his skin. Elco stumbled from the Humvee, pulled off his Kevlar helmet and flak vest. His ABUs. Hearing the commotion Chapo ran back to the Humvee, reached in the cabin and shut-off the motor, the engine coughing to a stop and then nothing but quiet. Elco stood shirtless, pants around his ankles—Elco's shadow a long and skinny alien beside him. Chapo picked up Elco's helmet and flung it back to him. "Shit Elco, you took his head right off."

The makeshift divider Elco had seen from the street was part of a mishmash shrine in the middle of Chapo's backyard, crude walls and a camo-net roof. Leaving Perla inside the shrine, Chapo came and sat beside Elco. The snow had turned soft, flakes gently floating from the gray sky.

"I hear you need a hospital, Private," Chapo said.

"Just a little rest," Elco said. "Where's Perla?"

"She's in there with Chapito, my boy. I told her I'd bring you over to see the saguaro. That it has healed before." Chapo took a deep breath. "You look like you did at the war. Like shit. Didn't the army tell you the war was over?"

"You're the one still in uniform. Still giving the orders."

"What do you want me to say, Private? Apologize for wanting to clear that ridge? For saving the water supply? Sorry you feel bad about what had to be done. If it makes you feel better, you were just following orders."

"That's always made me feel worse," Elco said.

Chapo laughed, and Chapito, with his hunting rifle

across his chest, walked from the shrine and stood by his father. Elco recognized the way he eyed the remaining crowd as they lit candles and left prayer cards, buried small boxes with crosses on them, the boy unsure how to spot the difference between a friendly and an enemy as he glanced at Elco and his father.

Chapo unpinned a photograph from his red robe and handed it to Elco. The photo was peeling at the corners; the image was of a young man in service dress, the glossy paper cracked and faded, the Airman probably long dead. "That was my abuelo," Chapo said. "He used to load bombs. He's the reason I signed up in the first place."

"I'm sure he was proud," Elco said, rubbing the picture between his fingers.

"He wasn't. He didn't want me in this shit from the start, but I wasn't too good at listening," Chapo said.

"I remember."

"What happened to being the quiet type? I used to like that about you, Private."

"You were the only one," Elco said. "I need to check on Perla."

He tried to hand back Chapo's photograph but was waved off, Chapo saying he was tired of carrying the old man around. Chapo disappeared inside the house, his son, too. Elco put the photograph in his pocket and felt Perla's book inside the lining, remembered he was wearing her coat. How cold she must be without it. Elco read the title, Pedro Páramo; the red cover had Perla's name carved along the bottom. Lorna had written on the title page, her letters looping over the bold print: Mija, This book contains all of us. Every last word. Elco thumbed through the pages, watched them flip until he reached the last; he read the final lines: After a few steps he fell; inside, he was begging for help, but no words were audible. He fell to the ground with a thud, and lay there, collapsed like a pile of rocks.

Elco waited for Perla by the entrance to the shrine. The saguaro was more than twenty feet tall with thick, curved arms, each lined with sharp spines. The light green skin was scarred with holes made by woodpeckers that had once picked through the peel until reaching the wooden bones underneath. Snowflakes fell through the netting and melted on the Christmas lights. The bulbs flickered on-and-off. Buzzed. A crown of white flowers circled the head of the cactus, the long buds opened like bells.

Soon it would be night, the cold coming harder than before, but Elco wanted Perla to take her time. To finish the story she was working on. Perla stood with her arms wrapped around her belly, and Elco imagined she was feeling for her baby's arms and legs growing inside, a tiny heart beating alongside her own. Elco collapsed to the ground. He lied still, unable to move but certain he could hear the little heart beating, faint at first but becoming louder: thump-thump, thump-thump, thump-thump.

Acknowledgements

Without the love of my wife, Marlo, this book would not be possible, and I'm not sure where or who I would be. Thank you, and I love you.

Versions of the stories collected here have appeared in the following journals: Alligator Juniper, Bordersenses, Cutthroat, Huizache, Moonshot Magazine, PALABRA, PANK, The Acentos Review, and The Literary Review. I truly appreciate the generosity and enthusiasm of the editors of these wonderful literary spaces. I would especially like to thank Rachel Yoder, Minna Proctor, Beth Alvarado, Amit Ghosh, Elena Minor, and Diana López.

I owe a tremendous debt, admiration and gratitude, to the teachers who encouraged, guided and befriended me along the way: Aurelie Sheehan, Buzz Poverman, Meg Files, Jennifer Jenkins, Alison Deming, Elizabeth Evans, Jason Brown, Joy Baggett, and Elroy Bode. Thank you, as always. And I owe an even greater debt to my co-workers and friends at the Arizona Air National Guard. Without their help my education would have been impossible. Thanks to everyone who picked up the slack when I missed work to make workshops.

A special thanks to my literary hermano Manuel Muñoz whose work inspires and challenges me, whose generosity is appreciated more than he knows. Dagoberto Gilb, your friendship and guidance have been invaluable.

Twitching Heart

Finally I wish to thank my family, my Má and Pops (Connie and Joe), my sister Christine and brother Tony. I carry you all with me always, as I do our city, Chuco, the very center of whom I am and where these stories come from.

About the Author

Matt Méndez's stories have appeared in *Alligator Juniper, Cutthroat, Huizache, PALABRA, PANK, The Literary Review* and other journals. Originally from El Paso he lives in Tucson where he also works as an aircraft mechanic. *Twitching Heart* is his first book. Contact him at matt@mattmendez.com

About the Cover Artist

Mario Robert is an artist from El Paso, Texas. His work is a mix of many Southwestern flavors seasoned with West Coast and Pacific Northwest influences. Contact him at roetairbroom@yahoo.com.

Made in the USA
Middletown, DE
12 January 2020